AFRICAN WRITERS SERIES

Editorial Adviser · Chinua Achebe

86

AGATHA MOUDIO'S SON

AFRICAN WRITERS SERIES

AGATHA MOUDIO'S SON

FRANCIS BEBEY

Translated by
JOYCE A. HUTCHINSON

HEINEMANN
NAIROBI · LONDON · IBADAN

Heinemann Educational Books Ltd
48 Charles Street, London W1X 8AH
PMB 5205 Ibadan · POB 25080 Nairobi
EDINBURGH MELBOURNE AUCKLAND TORONTO
HONG KONG SINGAPORE NEW DELHI

ISBN 0 435 90086 2

First published in French by Editions CLE, Yaoundé,
Cameroun as *Le Fils d'Agatha Moudio* 1967
First published in English translation 1971

Printed in Great Britain by
Cox & Wyman Ltd, London, Fakenham and Reading

1

Our village clustered at the foot of the hill from where the grey road led down from the distant town. The morning wore the sunny garb of a holiday, the peaceful calm of a June Sunday. Peace continued to reign until, suddenly, a shot rang out, followed shortly after by two or three more. However, although they seemed to come right out of the blue, nobody in the village was worried by these shots. They were coming from the near-by forest. Nobody paid any attention to them; nobody, that is, but Moudiki. What reason had he to upset himself on account of these shots fired far from our village when the other villagers remained utterly indifferent to them?

Moudiki came in.

'You heard them arrive, Mbaka?' he asked, closing the door behind him. 'You heard their car arrive?'

'Certainly I heard them arrive. Do you think I'm deaf? I even heard two or three of their shots a moment ago. They are already hunting. Ekéké is with them, I suppose?'

'Yes, Ekéké is with them,' replied Moudiki.

Then he fell silent. He still had something else to say but he was reluctant to speak. It was a bit tricky, the kind of question he wanted to ask. The two men looked at each other in silence for a moment, each one thinking things over for himself. Finally, Moudiki made up his mind:

'All the same there's something that bothers me, Mbaka,' he said.

'Something bothering you? What is it?'

'Listen, Mbaka, you are the Chief of our village, the Chief of us all. You mustn't deceive us. I have come to ask you what the position is about those people.'

'What, the position about those people? What do you mean? I don't understand you.'

'What I mean to say, what I mean is . . . Tell me: if I put the question frankly, you won't get angry?'

'Why should I get angry?'

Mbaka was more and more intrigued. It must be something serious. Why should Moudiki come and see him this Sunday morning and suddenly behave in such a mysterious and guarded manner, when ordinarily he was the very personification of straightforwardness and good spirits?

'No, I won't get angry. Ask your question, I'll answer you . . . if it's possible to answer,' said Chief Mbaka.

'Very well then, here goes: tell me, these whites who come hunting in our area, have they given you anything?'

'Given me anything? How do you mean?'

'Yes, you know what I mean: have they given you compensation?'

'Compensation? How?'

'If I've got it right,' insisted Moudiki, 'haven't they given you a little . . . you know, a little money?'

'Money? Really, sometimes you talk as if you didn't want people to understand you: what money? What for?'

'Chief Mbaka, I have always thought that you were a bit lacking in common sense, but this time, I'm sure I'm right. I'll explain what I mean: those people, they don't belong around here; they're strangers. If they come hunting here, we can't let them do it free of charge. They ought to pay something, and you know, they . . .'

'I'm interrupting, Moudiki, because there's one thing

2

you're beginning to forget, with your common sense. You're beginning to forget that it is those people who rule us, you, me, all the villagers, just as they rule our forest, our stream, our river, and all the animals and fish that live in them. Then you tell me how you would go about asking people like that to pay you money, just because they go hunting in the forest?'

'That's true, Mbaka, and I've thought about it as well. But they are the people who invented money. *They* manufacture it. They have plenty for themselves. So they must have some to spare for us too ... I ... mean: to offer us a little, out of friendship, at least to give us the impression that they like to come hunting here. Don't you think it would be reasonable ... and fair, to suggest that they should give us a little present from time to time? For all of us, Mbaka, not just for me. You are the chief and you ought to think of that, for the sake of your people. I repeat that it's not just for myself but for all of us.'

Mbaka went and sat on an old chair, near the window, put his head in his hands and began to think. Why, oh why had he not thought of his people since the whites had started to come hunting in our forest? In his heart of hearts Mbaka acknowledged the justice of Moudiki's proposal.

'Yes, you're right,' he said finally. 'You're perfectly right, Moudiki. These people can't come hunting here like that without ever giving us anything.'

'*You* say "anything", but *I* mean "money",' corrected Moudiki. 'You must speak to them about it this very day. And if they refuse, you can tell them not to come hunting monkeys in our district any more. Don't forget that you are the Chief: you shouldn't be afraid of whites.'

Moudiki was the kind of man who knows how to bring pressure to bear by using arguments. Mbaka was very well acquainted with this aggressive type. He was well aware that

Moudiki didn't often have really brilliant ideas, but that when he did happen to have one, nothing would persuade him to give it up, no matter what risks might be involved in putting it into practice. However, unlike the other times when he had fought tooth and nail to oppose Moudiki's proposals, it was not from a desire to please his morning visitor that today Mbaka admitted that Moudiki was right: he really thought so. Money was important. He would talk to the whites about it, all the more readily because the other inhabitants of the village would hold it against him terribly if one day they learned that he, their Chief, had been afraid to ask the hunters to compensate the community.

'All right,' said the Chief, 'I'll go and see them this very day, and I'll ask them for money.'

At this, Moudiki went back home again, congratulating himself on his initiative. Then the village continued to remain calm, as on any sunny Sunday morning.

At about four o'clock in the afternoon, Ekéké indicated the path leading out of the wood. All the village children were waiting for the hunters on the edge of the wood, and they went with them as far as their car. This had become the custom: every Sunday, at four o'clock in the afternoon, the children of Bonakwan, their numbers swollen by the children of the neighbouring village of Bonakamé, greeted the whites who had come from the town for their weekly hunting party. That day St Hubert had been particularly well-disposed. The hunters were about to get into their car, satisfied with their day, and happy to see the children of our district so happy with their visit, when Moudiki approached Ekéké:

'Tell your whites that Chief Mbaka has something to ask them.'

Ekéké translated into French, and the whites understood that the Chief wanted to see them.

4

'Why does he want to see us?' asked one of them.

'I don't know,' replied Ekéké. How could he know?'

'Very well, let him come here, the Chief, let him come here, if he wants to see us. But do tell him to hurry, because we're rather anxious to get home now. We're beginning to feel hungry.'

It was quite clear that they had no wish to waste their time. They looked at their watches several times. The Chief wants to see us . . . very well, he'll have to hurry.

Mbaka arrived without taking the time to fasten his cloth firmly round his loins. He must hurry, for the hunters were hungry. Nothing like a monkey-hunt to make you hungry. Moudiki knew this very well, but he also thought that the whites had no right to feel hungry unless they behaved properly towards us.

'Why do you want to see us, Chief?'

'To ask you for a little present for our village.'

'A little present? What does that mean?'

There were three white men and their two white women. We had often wondered, in the village, how three white men could be the husbands of two white women, but these people had their own way of life, so different from ours . . . And then, the two ladies always wore trousers: what kind of woman was this . . .? One of the men was very rich, at least we thought so every time he opened his mouth to speak, for he had replaced the two rows of ivory that heaven must surely have given him at birth with two sparkling rows of gold. He was tall and strong and ugly. What a strange man, we said among ourselves: and, in addition to all that, he had so much gold that he didn't know what to do with it, and was prepared to waste it by changing it into teeth. What a strange man . . .

The two ladies got into the car and began to wave fans with designs of many colours. The children were looking at these men and these women with curiosity and admiration;

especially the man with the gold-filled mouth, in spite of his strange ugliness. But why on earth weren't they black, like us?

'A little present? What does that mean?' asked one of them. He didn't understand.

'It means a little money,' said Mbaka, cupping his hand.

'What do you want it for, this money?'

'To buy a little salt for all the people of our village, to make sure the monkeys are still alive in the forest when you come back next time.'

'What on earth are you talking about?'

The request seemed so unwarranted to the hunter that he thought for a moment that my cousin Ekéké must have been mistranslating into French what Chief Mbaka was saying in his native tongue. But it was exactly what the Chief was saying. In any case, what was so incomprehensible about it?

'What is he talking about?' asked another white. 'He wants to make us pay for his monkeys now? What's more, I say "*his* monkeys" as if they belonged to him. He wants to make us pay for monkeys that we have caught ourselves, and which are of no use to us?'

Each one of us, naturally, was wondering what they did with all the monkeys that they came and killed in our forest. In our village, nobody used this breed of animal with a human head for food. But we were convinced that for them, on the other hand, it was a delicacy. In any case, why were they hungry at this time of day? Simply because they had not yet eaten, that was clear. And why had they not yet eaten? Because they were waiting to eat until they got back from hunting. So you tell me: what were they going to do when they got home? Leave these monkeys plucked from the trees in the most overpowering tropical heat to rot on the rubbish-heap? What a likely tale!

The whole village had arrived in the square, having heard that the Chief had something to say to the whites. When a Chief has something to say, it's an event; for his prestige is at

6

stake. Mbaka had come to the meeting with the white hunters well aware that if his plan failed he would have to shut himself up in his house for several days, and that he could no longer expect to be obeyed, or to get an order of any kind carried out. What demon had inspired Moudiki to suggest this meeting, then, Mbaka wondered. At all events, now that everybody was gathered round the car, surrounding the strangers to the village, the Chief could no longer draw back. Moreover, as they had come in such numbers, Mbaka knew that his people all intended to support him, since he was making the request for the good of the whole community.

'What's this all about?'

'It's about salt, sir,' replied Mbaka.

Our visitors thought they were dealing with savages. They were mistaken, for, in the outlying suburbs of Douala, we were the descendants of Bilé, son of Bessengué, the man who had once astonished all the tribes of Douala by his unrivalled riches, and who reigned over the tribe of the Akwas 'for centuries', even after his death. We could not therefore be afraid of whites, even if they carried guns. This was what I was thinking when, furious at having been held up by a tale of cooking-salt, about which he refused to understand anything, one of the hunters said to Mbaka, rudely:

'You won't get it, the salt for your tribe. We owe you nothing. We come here to hunt monkeys, which belong to nobody. What's more, without us and our guns the colony of monkeys in your forest would cause you plenty of trouble, even in your village. We are benefactors, and it's you, in fact, who should consider paying us something, instead of wasting our time when we're hungry . . .'

At this point I intervened.

'We're wasting your time? Perhaps you think that because you carry guns we shall be afraid to ask you for compensation if you come hunting in our forest. Well, I assure you that you won't leave here with these monkeys, unless you do as Chief Mbaka asks ... Ekéké, translate what I have just said for them.'

I elbowed my way through the assembled crowd and stationed myself in front of the three white men. They looked at me and found they were looking at a stone wall. But their surprise seemed to stem above all from the fact that probably for the first time in their lives an African villager had dared to address them in this precise and aggressive manner. I had to force myself to hide my pleasure when I saw how greatly impressed they were not only by my build, but still more by the terms in which I had spoken to them. All the inhabitants of the village were proud of me. Just think: for them I represented times long since vanished in the dark night of ages and of injustice. I was a true son of Bilé son of Bessengué. I was the son of this village, which could count quite a few glorious exploits in its history. In any case, for the past three or four years everybody's eyes had been fixed on me: the wrestling bouts against the surrounding villages had given me a chance to show off my muscular strength, and I was in the process of gradually becoming a legend, just like the great wrestlers of our people who had gone before.

Then the white hunters looked at each other, as if for guidance, without saying a word. But they were hungry, and that cut short all the rest. One after another, they raised their hats to me, then, awkwardly, put their hands in their pockets, and brought out . . . yes indeed, genuine coins. And they gave them to *me* and *I* handed them to Chief Mbaka. No need to tell you of my pride in this moment of glory.

Then, one of the whites, suddenly remembering that he could write, took a notebook out of some pocket or other about his person and asked who I was. Now my cousin Ekéké worked on a very laudable principle; when he was interpreting for the village, he translated everything that was said to him, the lot, including proper names. So, when I replied that my name was Mbenda, my cousin seized the opportunity to show his zeal:

'He is called the Law,' he said.

'What did you say?' I asked my cousin. 'What did you tell the white man? Repeat what you have just told him about my name.'

'I told him you are called the Law,' he answered; 'that is what Mbenda means in French.'

Ekéké must have been right, for the man he was speaking to began again immediately, talking to me:

'That's right, the Law, that's right, that's the way ... You'll be hearing from me.'

That is how the name stuck, for everybody in our village immediately found himself the richer for a new word, and moreover, a French word: *La Loi*.

As for the man's last remark, spoken in such friendly tones, all my family immediately thought that I should certainly be offered a job in the town. And off they went swollen with envy, saying that I was the luckiest child of the village. People will reason like this ... They couldn't even see how much I disliked the idea of giving up my happy life as a fisherman, in order to wear trousers, a shirt and a tie. At all events, the supposedly happy outcome foreseen by my prophetic brothers failed to materialize. In fact, a week after this day full of cooking-salt and promises for the future, we had a visit, unexpected, to say the least, from M. Dubous, Commissioner of Police for Douala. If I had had the spirit to go out to sea fishing on that day, I should no doubt have avoided many complications. I don't understand why I was lazy and stayed in the village. I didn't put out to sea and I gained fifteen days' detention in the prison at New-Bell. Fifteen days' detention, without trial, for having dared to ask for money for the cooking salt needed by our community – this was the rate at the time. The law had so ordained.

9

2

Agatha Moudio had taken some precautions before coming to visit me: she had thrown a whole handful of salt into the kitchen fire. At Douala, everybody knows how to make it rain; you merely burn a little salt, and immediately the heavens open as in the days of Noah's Ark. And not just a little shower, against which any old raincoat will protect you. No, real, rainy-season rain, water falling from the sky in thick, fat drops, when no one dares venture out.

Agatha came in and made me think furiously: what would Maa Médi say if she found this girl with me, alone with me? If only she had come on a weekday, it wouldn't have mattered much: my mother went to work in the fields every day, and the few gossips who might have made it their business to report to her that Agatha had been to see me would certainly not have succeeded in convincing her. But today, a Sunday afternoon when everybody was in the village, was not the day to choose to visit me, even though the visit did overwhelm me with joy.

'You mustn't stay here long,' I said to Agatha, 'you mustn't . . .'

I had hardly finished saying this when the clapping began on the roof of my house, so suddenly and so loud that I had to stop, taken aback. The burnt-salt trick had obviously been a great success.

'All the same you can't turn me out in such a downpour,' replied Agatha, assuming an expression of sublime innocence.

'No, certainly not,' I said, with a glance that said plenty: I was sure that it was she who had made it rain to prevent the village asking questions about her presence in my house. Now, there was no danger of Maa Médi, whose house was two back from mine, coming to see for herself that Agatha was with me.

'What rain . . .' she said, coming nearer.

The outcome of our meeting was decisive, as you will see later on. But today, on this Sunday when it was raining so hard, I was face to face with a child of seventeen who was already getting herself talked about in a way that few people manage in a whole lifetime. I would never wish any girl of any country to have the reputation of Agatha Moudio. In our village, as in hers, quite near-by, as well as in all the villages of the district, it was generally thought that the extraordinary beauty of this 'creature of Satan' disguised all the evil that she was already capable of. Imagine that, at her age, she already knew 'everything'; give to this expression a pejorative meaning which would shock the morals of the whole world, and you will understand perhaps why Maa Médi was unwilling to see me enter into intimate relations with Agatha: 'She already knows men,' they said when speaking of her. And often, they were more explicit: 'She goes to the European quarter of the town every day; that's why she's always well dressed.' People, naturally, exaggerated a little. Nevertheless, Agatha was so notorious in her way that I would never have dared to hope that she would one day fall in love with me. But when that happened I was so happy about it that I immediately forgot everything I had heard said about Agatha. I believe that any of the men of our village, any of those who said the nastiest things about her would have reacted as I did. Men are like that. When a woman tells them she loves them they waste no time in forgetting, so that they can forgive and be loved.

Agatha's love for me dated from the famous day when I

had dared to tell the white hunters that they would not leave our village with the monkeys from our forest if they didn't pay what Chief Mbaka was asking: a little money for salt for our community. The voice of courage reaches the heart. Agatha was there, in the square, at the time of that unforgettable encounter. Like everybody else, she had admired my determination; more than anybody else, she had appreciated my naked torso shining in the sun, my courage, everything which had persuaded the hunters to consider the request of our village chief. More than anybody, she had admired me. 'And I would have liked to tell you so, or simply to make you understand at that very moment,' she was to confess to me later, 'but I couldn't do so, there were so many people round you.' What were all those people doing round me just at that moment, I wonder? Then I went to spend a fortnight at New-Bell; a fortnight during which I was employed in various forms of hard labour, cleaning the town on behalf of the colonial administration. Agatha came to see me in prison from time to time, and brought me parcels of budding love and ripe oranges. I shall never forget that time: I suddenly discovered that the girl who was the target for all eyes in the two or three neighbouring villages loved me, me and only me. Prison became a little more bearable because of it, in spite of the inhuman treatment to which I was almost continually subjected during my stay. And people went on saying that Agatha was not a girl, but the devil incarnate . . . On leaving prison, I decided to break with the generally accepted, and absurd, principle, according to which no reasonable man should dream of having serious relations with this young girl. I went to talk to Maa Médi about it.

'Young girl, young girl,' replied my mother. 'You really imagine you are dealing with a young girl, simply because she brought you some oranges when you were in prison?'

'Maa, I'm sure she's as pure as any other girl, whether of our village or hers . . .'

'Who told you they were pure? Who told you that? My son, if your father were still alive, he would tell you that there are no pure girls any more these days. Get that into your head once and for all: purity, that was in my day. Except even today, there are girls who still have some self-respect. They don't all behave like Agatha; they don't go and parade in the European quarter waiting to be picked up by the first white man they meet. As for me, I would never wish to have as a daughter-in-law a creature like that, who is quite simply a disgrace to her family. Her father, you know her father . . . he lets her wander around because he's had enough of her.'

I kept silent.

Then Maa Médi went on, after pausing for breath:

'And now, her father doesn't know what to think about her any more. He thinks that if she is what she is, it can't be natural. He thinks there is a sorcerer behind it who is leading his daughter astray, and he hopes to lay his hands on the evil spirit one day. But believe me: the day that he's convinced there is no evil spirit influencing his daughter, you will see him turn Agatha out of his house. Just you wait and see. For the moment, she's no great catch, and you don't want to go saddling yourself with soiled goods . . .'

'Maa, stop saying that, Agatha isn't what . . .'

'You tell me that she isn't what people say? It's not for me to remind you of all her escapades: apart from her visits to the European quarter, you seem to forget her inexplicable affair with Headman, the road foreman. A man like that, a man who is nothing and has nothing, and who isn't even a local . . . Agatha lets herself be taken off by him, and you tell me she isn't what I think, and that she doesn't deserve that I should keep you away from her?'

Maa Médi was right. I hadn't thought of the scandal that

Agatha had caused some time before, when it became known that she had been 'taken up' by Headman. Nobody in our village could excuse that. A respectable young girl doesn't let herself be taken up by just anybody. And Headman, who was merely a road-worker, and who worked on his feet all day, even out in the rain when it was raining, and who in addition hadn't even the advantage of being a 'local', Headman was just anybody. It had been a disgusting affair. I remembered, hearing Maa Médi recall it to my mind, the shame we had all felt at the idea that a descendant of Bilé, son of Bessengué, had fallen so low, dragging in the mud the memory of our incomparable ancestor. In our village, we had consoled ourselves by saying that, after all, Agatha's people belonged to a quite different branch of the genealogical tree from the one we were descended from. We had held fast to this way of explaining the 'extravagant behaviour of the girls of Bonakamé' and thanks to this philosophy . . . of escapism, we had gradually managed to persuade ourselves that the scandal only concerned us at a distance. As I say, a disgusting affair. I wonder why Agatha's father didn't turn her out afterwards. And there, in front of my mother, I felt the sweat running down my forehead, merely at the memory of the escapade with Headman.

'It's true, Maa,' I said, 'it's true, I had forgotten all that.'

I wiped my brow. Maa Médi swallowed, satisfied. Her son had not yet reached the point of disobeying her, as was often the case with those bad boys who imagined that at twenty-two they could do as they pleased. Maa Médi thought over my disappointment and took pity on me; but she had not the slightest intention of giving way. You know what she said: 'I would never want a creature like that for a daughter-in-law. . . .' You, who know Maa Médi, you know that she really meant what she had just said, and that nothing on earth would make her change her mind. Nothing on earth . . . but wait for the end of my story before you swear to it.

For Maa Médi, I was the only son of a husband who had died leaving to his wife nothing but his only son, and no other fortune. For her, I was all that is good in life, and I had to be kept good and pure all my life. 'He is the apple of her eye,' they said, talking of me and my mother. Everything she did in the world was done for my happiness. However, she would not have allowed me, for a moment, to think that I would ever be a spoilt child: 'If you don't like school,' she used to tell me when I was a child, 'if you don't like school, you won't go to school. But, my son, you will have to earn your own living, by any honest means. Don't count on me to help you become a ne'er-do-well, no matter how much I love you.' I didn't like school and I didn't go to school; at least, I stopped going as soon as I knew how to count. The fresh air and the high seas were calling me, and I quickly said goodbye to the benches, to classmates more patient than I, and to the blackboard, which I shall never forget. At fifteen I became a fisherman, and from that age I experienced the extraordinary adventure of deep-sea fishing, with mountainous waves, and the frail craft at the mercy of God, and evenings smelling of smoked fish, and the comradeship of brave men, with the common aim of maintaining lives of other men, at the risk of their own lives. I was a brave man and the pride of my mother, to whom it was reported that I was the strongest of the fishermen of my age. And since she had decided that I was a man, a real man, Maa Médi had made for herself a picture of me which she wished to be permanent: 'You are not a rich man's son who does everything he likes, simply because he has money, and nothing he does will shock anybody. No, you are simply my child, and the most worthy son of this village and of the district. And what you do will shock everybody if it is not well done, for you will have no money to close mouths and to stop evil tongues wagging . . .' My mother repeated this every time she thought I had strayed from the path of what she and 'the other people' called duty. I could not disobey Maa Médi. She was my mother, with all that implies of respect and gratitude. I lost my father when I was not more than six or seven. 'He loved you very much,' Maa Médi always told me. It's true, he loved me very much, he had often confided as much to one of his friends, Tanga. And Tanga, after the death of my father, a long time after even, never stopped telling everybody, whenever he found me with other people, that in all his life he had never seen paternal love as great as that of my poor father for me. It must be true: hadn't my father, before he died, and even before it was time to think of dying, given some thought to the woman that I should marry later on? No, he had not written the name of my future wife in his will; my father would in any case have had some difficulty with this, for as far as I know he had not been to school and therefore couldn't write. But in our society, the finest written will had hardly the same authority as the words spoken by a man on the point of death. The spoken word means life, life which goes on, which man must respect at all times, because it is the only thing here below that never fades. Men who can write lose this profound respect for life. They know that their thoughts will not be debased with the passage of time: they know that what they say or think today will be the same tomorrow, no matter who lives after them: the written word remains and gives a permanent shape to their thoughts. In this way, the spoken word, the natural manifestation of life, is replaced by a completely conventional invention of men, the written word. It is then easy to understand how life itself loses some of its importance, and to explain world wars decimating millions of men, or, on a more modest scale, but showing no more respect for life, robbery with violence.

By inventing writing, man thought to protect himself from the ravages of time: he has locked up his thoughts in the book, to which he accords an increasing confidence which nothing seems able to destroy. And yet the book in no way deserves this excess of confidence for it is, fundamentally, the most indiscreet of friends: tell it that you have just made a discovery and it forthwith sets about divulging it to the world, as if the matter concerned the whole world. This system of having no secrets from anyone is in the end the best way of not informing anyone, since everybody knows very well that what is written is not intended for him, personally.

In our society, we had preserved the ancestral custom of communicating things only to those we loved, and with the certainty that they would make good use of our information. That is why the spoken word kept – and still keeps today – an importance that will not quickly be usurped by the newspaper and the book. The spoken word becomes even more powerful at the hour of death, when words become sacred commands.

And I was there with Maa Médi to hear her remember what my father had said a few seconds before he died.

'. . . for you will have no money to close mouths and to stop evil tongues wagging,' she said.

Then she waited a while before going on:

'In any case, you know that your father, your poor father who left you when you were still only a child, you know that he had found you a bride before he died.'

It was true: my father, before drawing his last breath, had had the strength to find me a wife for later on, when I was grown up: 'Listen, Tanga, if ever one of your wives has a daughter one day, I beg you, give her as a wife to my son; you hear me, Tanga?' And Tanga, weeping, had answered yes, seeing that his friend's eyes were closing for ever. So it was that at the age of six I was already betrothed, although my future wife had not yet even been conceived in her mother's womb. Some three years passed before she saw the light of day: it was Fanny, the first daughter of Tanga's wife, or rather of his third wife; for, seeing that neither of the two wives that he had at the time of my father's death had managed to bear a daughter, Tanga, out of friendship for my father, took a third wife, who finally gave him a fiancée for me.

Fanny was now thirteen. I was twenty-two. I wonder why I mechanically made this mental comparison, coming to the conclusion that Agatha, who was a little more than seventeen, would certainly be a more suitable wife for me than Fanny. But Maa Médi was watching me closely. There was between her and me an invisible thread, linking our two minds from morning till evening, so that my mother could see clearly all that I kept hidden in the depths of my inmost thoughts. I was therefore surprised to hear her say, as if she too had made the same mental comparison of the three different ages, and as if she wanted to answer the questions that this comparison might lead me to ask:

'You know, you can't refuse to marry her just because she's only thirteen . . . on the contrary, her age is an asset for you. A wife, my son, can be trained. Take her while she is still quite young and you will have plenty of time to train her in the way you want and make of her a wife exactly suited to your needs. At thirteen, she is not too young to marry, believe me. And then, tell me, what hurry is there to be married immediately? You can well wait another year or two, and marry when Fanny is fifteen. I was that age myself, when your father married me . . .'

That was where our differences began. For I no longer intended to wait a year or two before getting married. I wanted to do it as soon as possible. I think I would have done so immediately, if Maa Médi had given me permission to marry Agatha Moudio. There are times when a man experiences such a strong desire to cut a dash with a female companion of somewhat doubtful character that he becomes deaf to the advice of his own mother. And little by little, I became deaf to the advice of Maa Médi, at least in the matter of the long wait which she wanted to impose on me. 'Deaf' is a figure of speech, which does not exactly correspond to reality; for the child that I remained in the eyes of my mother would have found it difficult to disobey her, after the strict upbringing he had had, and its effects, particularly in the field of sexuality, of which he was almost entirely ignorant, were later to have unforeseeable consequences. We shall come to all that later. For the present, just listen to me:

'If I marry Fanny because I must,' I said, 'very well, I will, Maa. Only, wait another two years, that I will not.'

I don't know, myself, what made me in such a hurry. Today, it even seems ridiculous that I wanted at all costs to get married as soon as possible, just when my mother was of the opposite opinion: it is even more ridiculous, since I was not very sure what a man did with a woman once he had married her. At all events, that was my answer to Maa Médi that day: I had made a stand, and wasn't going to compromise. I hoped in this way to force my mother to admit that I needed a wife, immediately, and a wife who was already a woman, not a child-wife. It was a forlorn hope, but I persisted in this naïve way of thinking: I told myself that I could perhaps persuade Maa Médi to agree that this 'wife who was already a woman' was Agatha. I need hardly tell you that my mother saw through my scheme straight away. She assumed a completely unconcerned expression to defeat me:

'If you want her immediately, my son, nothing is easier, since her father is only waiting for a word from us.'

Maa Médi's position was clearly defined. My good mother remained the more faithful to the last wishes of her husband because she considered Agatha as the one girl in the world to whom I must never propose marriage.

At present, while the rain confined Agatha to my house, I was remembering the day when my mother had made me clearly understand that she didn't wish to see me with her. However, although I wanted to obey my mother as much as in the past, I don't think any sorcerer in the world could ever have helped me to do as she wished now, that is to say, to give up Agatha Moudio, to wait for Fanny, or else to marry her immediately if I so wished, and in that case to take charge of her training myself. There, face to face with Agatha, I felt even more incapable than ever of following my mother's advice. She bewitched me, literally; and while the thunder rolled outside, I realized fully that I loved this girl more than words could say, far more than Maa Médi herself could ever have guessed.

Naturally, I had not spoken to Agatha of my mother's opposition, and although she herself suspected it, she nevertheless made suggestions for the future, for 'our future'. We should be happy, and we mustn't pay attention to what people might say, for people's tongues were only too ready to wag about things that didn't concern them; and she would find a way of pleasing my mother, whom she liked a lot; and we should have children, a lot of children, just as in the legend of Bilé, son of Bessengué, our common ancestor; and then, who could tell? Perhaps one day I could become something more than a simple fisherman. At this point, I interrupted her:

'You know,' I told her, 'I am a fisherman because I myself chose to be one. It is the job I like and also the only one I can do well. I have no plans for becoming anything else. I like to walk around in the bright sunshine, wearing my wide loincloth, thanking heaven for creating me big and strong. I should hate to be a clerk, and anyway I doubt if I ever could be one, seeing how little time I spent at school. But at all events, I should like you to give up the idea that I shall one day change my job, to enter a supposedly better-paid profession: I like what I do in life, and indeed, I think the open air suits me very well.'

'And when we are married, you'll still go off on the high seas, on the treacherous seas . . . for weeks and weeks . . . and you'll leave me all alone here?'

I answered that such was the fate of many other women in our village and that they were none the worse for it. You see what I meant when I told you earlier that I didn't yet know what marriage was . . . I sensed that Agatha was somewhat disappointed. But when, a few minutes later, she began to tell me her life story, I understood what lay behind her desire to become one day what is generally called 'somebody'; I understood also that she was disappointed by my frankness and above all by my determination not to improve my social position. She needed a husband whom she could love all her life; but at the same time she wouldn't object if he had one of those stable and secure positions which ensure peace of mind by means of a wallet filled regularly at the end of each month. But I think she loved me more than that, for her disappointment was passing and she never referred to it in our subsequent conversations. However that may be, this rainy day gave me the chance to get to know Agatha Moudio better.

'You know,' she told me, 'I am my mother's daughter rather than my father's.'

I didn't see what she was getting at. I smiled, to show that she had just uttered something like a proverb: a child can never be absolutely sure of anybody but its mother, unless it is an adopted child. To a certain extent, therefore, it is above all its mother's child, rather than its father's. Agatha understood my amused smile and explained herself:

'Don't laugh at me; you'll understand: My father, with his four wives, has never bothered about my existence, nor about my education. If I was able to go to school for a few years, if I grew up and became the person you see now, I owe it to my mother. The poor woman had had three children by my father. My mother was my father's first wife.

A wife absolutely beyond reproach, believe me. Unfortunately, when the children began to appear, the two firstborn weren't boys. Well, you know how it is with us: a man who doesn't have a boy straight away gives his wife a second chance with the next child. But if the wife still doesn't manage to give her husband a boy, it's unforgivable. The husband is forced to take another wife, in the hope that this one will not fail to produce the longed-for boy.'

'That is what most men do,' I said.

I knew that I should perhaps one day be obliged to do the same thing. But the thought that I should perhaps do so, even if Agatha were my first wife, plunged me briefly in despair. Agatha had the same thought, I am sure: the silence which followed my remark convinced me. Outside, the sky was still dripping water. What weather . . .

'Yes, that's what most men do,' said Agatha at last with a sigh. 'It can't be otherwise, I admit, although it's difficult to make a baby a boy or girl to order. As for my father, I have to agree that he behaved pretty well towards my mother, for he even gave her a third chance. That was when I came into the world. I whom my father was not expecting, since he wanted a boy. When I arrived he was furious. Nobody had ever seen such anger at the birth of a child. My mother once told me that my father refused to see me, during the first two or three months of my life, and that people from my mother's family went to entreat him to forgive me for having been born. They took a cock with white feathers, two kids, two huge yams and a 500-franc note, which they gave to my father to reconcile him to my arrival. The reconciliation took place at a feast attended by members of both families. But naturally, my father held it against my mother too. He despised her just as much as he had previously loved her. Men are like that, they can't forgive their wives for disappointing them. For you know, during my mother's third pregnancy my father was so sure that the child she was expecting would be a boy that he invited friends from a distance a few days before the birth. You can imagine the faces of all these people who had been looking forward to my birth; imagine their expressions when I presented to them the innocent little face of a new-born child that nobody wanted, nobody, except my poor mother; for her part, she remembered that she had carried me in her womb for nearly ten months.'

'But,' I interrupted, 'didn't your mother benefit at all from the reconciliation and the feasting?'

'You don't know my father,' said Agatha. 'He didn't hold it against me any more, so to speak, but you know, at bottom, he has never completely forgiven me. As for mother, he made life harder and harder for her, and if the poor woman died at the end of a long illness, the ill-treatment that my father inflicted on her did nothing to help her recover, believe me. I am convinced that she died of grief as much as from illness.'

'That was three years ago . . .'

'Yes, she has been dead three years. I was a bit more than fourteen when my mother died. Since then, I have been left to my own devices. And all alone, I grew up, oh yes, I grew up, I can tell you.'

I had no difficulty in believing her; all that was said about her was not unknown to me. But now, I could see better, in my mind, the succession of events: it was in fact in the last two or three years that this little girl had become the most notorious person in the district; so it was after her mother's death that alone, or almost alone in the world, with a father who paid more attention to his three other wives and to his 'boy children', that she had gradually acquired her reputation, a very bad reputation. That was what our people had not yet realized: Agatha's bad behaviour was the result of a bad upbringing, left to chance. Therefore, to make this poor girl responsible for mistakes which she would not have made if she had had a more intelligent father, seemed to me grossly unfair.

Evening had fallen under the pouring rain.

Salt, I said to myself, she burnt salt before coming, but I bet she threw a whole shovelful on the fire. What rain, heavens, what rain . . . Agatha went on talking, softly, explaining, or rather laying bare her life, and her way of seeing the future. And this girl, who was by no means a mature person, staggered me by the lucidity of what she said. She was an intelligent girl, and it gave me more than pleasure to realize it:

'You see, I have not led a normal life . . .'

'Come now, Agatha, you talk as if you were already an old woman of seventy, who takes a fleeting glance into the depths of her past, and suddenly finds that she has not lived as she should or could have lived. Life? It's before you.'

'Before us, if you will,' she said.

I trembled at this invitation, thinking of Maa Médi.

'I didn't see things this way before,' Agatha went on; 'I must tell you the truth about this. I used to tell myself that, after such an unhappy childhood, I should meet a rich man, who would never think of taking a second wife once we were married, even if I couldn't give him a son; I was perhaps looking for a man who would make me happy as I had never been happy, but above all I wanted him to be rich, dressed in trousers, a shirt, a tie, a jacket, and with fine shoes on his feet; and then somebody, I don't know who, put into my head the idea that this young man would go and work in an office, with whites. And now, it doesn't matter any more, since I have found my man. He will do what he wants to do in life; I just want to stay near him. My future will from now on be yours, *La Loi*. You shall do with me what you wish, if you will take me for your wife.'

She was silent.

When a woman gets to this point in her story, she falls silent. It's a manœuvre. It gives her time quickly to make sure that she hasn't gone too far, and prepares her for the sigh of relief which, she hopes, will precede the rest of the conversation. A sigh of relief, which she will utter if the opposite party shows himself anxious to accept the proposal that has just been made to him; but this sigh can become one of undeniable displeasure if the man addressed fails to respond favourably to the declaration. So you see the embarrassing situation in which I found myself. To give a positive answer to Agatha was to reject all the arguments of Maa Médi, who had already given me the reasons why she did not want a daughter-in-law of this kind. To give a negative reply was quite simply impossible. To give no answer at all? I didn't care for these deferred solutions: they do not solve problems. I was vaguer . . .

'The future is so mysterious, Agatha,' I said. 'Let us go on loving each other and we shall see that things will sort themselves out in time. And then, you are still young, you know very well that . . .'

'What? I'm still young? You mean that I'm too young to become your fiancée or your wife? I'm young, and I talk to you like an adult. And I say that if we marry, I will help you to become a man. I am too young for you; tell me, have you a girl older than me to marry? And then who said that you necessarily needed an old woman, as if you were already old yourself? No, I'll tell you: you will marry me, because you love me, and I love you more than any other woman in the world will ever love you.'

Agatha worried me a little by this way of announcing that I was going to marry *her* and no other woman. A certain unpleasant feeling crept up my spine as the young girl spoke with this air of complete assurance. I was a bit scared. I told myself that with a wife like that, the future would no doubt hold for me, among other surprises, that of having to reckon with the very forceful personality of my dear wife. To sum up, if I accepted Agatha, I mean, if I agreed to marry her, I was entering on a life for two, of a kind that my ancestors had never known. For in their time, they could certainly ignore the opinion of their wives if they failed to see any sense in it. But the African woman of modern times has something to say. I hope for her that she may offer her opinion at the right moment in the conversation so that her hundred-per-cent civilized husband, may take notice of the view she expresses. Everybody is entitled to benefit from progress. But in our village, at the time when I was faced with the serious problem of taking a wife, things had not reached this high level of European civilization, which preaches the absolute equality of men and women here below. Far from it. So it was that suddenly realizing that I had no wish to be a great pioneer of the emancipation of the African woman, I managed to convince myself that Agatha, even though I loved her very much, was perhaps not the wife I really needed, in the context of our little village. The thought that she was also not particularly popular in the village did nothing to encourage me further to approve of the kind of love she showed for me.

'Listen, Agatha,' I said, interrupting her, 'listen, you are talking to me just as the white women talk to their men. On Sundays when the hunters come here, I sometimes see how one of the ladies scolds her husband. You frighten me, for I believe you would do the same if we were married. Perhaps you talk like that because you know the whites, but here in our village you may know very well that a woman never says to a man: "You will marry me, I shall marry you . . ." And you also know that it doesn't depend on us but on our parents. You no longer have your mother; and I lost my father more than fifteen years ago; but that in no way means that we are alone in the world and able to come to any decision we like about our marriage: we still have to consult our respective families. My proposal is that we go on loving each other just as much as we do at present, and gradually, you'll see, things will sort themselves out. It will all sort itself out, you'll see, and later on you'll agree with me that my proposal was wiser.'

By now it was completely dark, but Agatha's rain went on falling. That it should rain during the day and prevent people from going out, that is understandable; but that it should go on raining at night, at a time when it's doing no harm to anybody, seems to me pointless. And the rain was there, beating on the roof of my house, in the single street of our village, and everywhere in the countryside around us.

'If it goes on raining like this,' said Agatha, 'the women won't need to go and draw water from the river tomorrow: all the receptacles lined up along the gutters must be full by now.'

I then remembered, suddenly, the crushing superiority of our village over those around it. A short time before, a public-fountain had been installed, 'and we have clean water now,' I said, 'and no more of that dirty river water like you others'. Agatha was annoyed:

'In our village,' she replied, 'we don't need these foreign things. Heaven created the river and the rainwater for our pleasure; we can use it as we please. And what's more,' she concluded, 'we don't need this fountain, which sows discord among the women wherever it's installed.'

Agatha was right: the fountain, since its installation in our village, had brought about a new way of life among the inhabitants. In countries where people are used to running water in their flats, they don't realize what a positive revolution is caused by a public stand-pipe installed in a little African village. This device, which brings running water to people who have not previously known it in this mechanical form, also keeps the users informed of all that is happening, not only in the region, but also in 'the whole world'. I have confidence in our people: they know all about events, great or small, which take place in any latitude. But men practically never possess the extraordinary gift for free information which our women have. If you want to know that Ebanda beat his wife last night as no woman was ever beaten by her husband, if you want to learn that old Eboumbou is going to take a third wife, and that she comes from the Bakokos and is thirty years younger than he, if you want to discover that the chief of the neighbouring district is dishonest because he has sold some land which didn't belong to him, if you want to learn all this, together with the commentaries provoked by these sensational news-items, then go to the fountain, and there you will appreciate progress at its true value.

'No,' repeated Agatha, 'we don't like this sort of device; which sows discord among us . . . If you think that the arguments in which the women indulge at the fountain, all about nothing, make the whites' water preferable to God's water . . .?'

It was true: sometimes there were disgraceful scenes at the public fountain. All over nothing at all. For example, the arrival of a woman in too much of a hurry to draw water when it wasn't her turn was enough to cause a riot, which often ended with torn dresses, and torn to such a point . . . Endalé will never confess what happened to her that morning when her husband was nagging her to bring his bath water. For it must be said that, since the installation of the public fountain, most of our men had started to pay scrupulous attention to notions of hygiene hitherto unheard of in our village. In particular, they had understood how dangerous it was to go and bathe in the 'dirty water' of the river. They forgot that this 'dirty water' had rendered valuable service to our village, without proving to be particularly dangerous, before the fountain existed. And as dandies of the new era, they expected their wives to go and fetch water for the toilet or the bath at home.

So that morning Endalé arrived at the fountain. In her hurry she failed to notice other women who had arrived before her. There were there, among others, aunt Adela, the wife of my uncle Big-Heart; and Dina, a neighbour with a shabby and insignificant appearance, who wanted at all costs to pass for somebody important. My uncle Big-Heart was the only man in our village who worked regularly in the town; and Dina, whose husband was a fisherman like most of our men, was terribly envious of aunt Adela; for this reason she never missed a chance to remind her, in a rather scornful tone, that she didn't come from a nearby village, but that my uncle had sought her far away, after days and nights of walking in the bush. I wonder why my uncle Big-Heart had sought my aunt after days and nights of walking so far in the bush?

And then that morning, there was also Mother Evil-Eye. Yes, she was there, 'naturally', you will say later, when you meet her again, for by then you will know that in our village she was to be found everywhere, at all hours of the day and night.

The tap was running, running, slowly, not caring for the passing of time. The water smelt of the new pipe. It was not clear; it had a whitish sediment which even today makes me doubt its cleanness. But for us, it was the water which came out of the public fountain, that is to say the water which had been treated by the whites 'specially to supply our village' as we used to say, not without pride. That was enough to make us prefer it to water from the best spring, no matter how clear and pure it might be. We were beginning to enter cheerfully on civilized life, such as had easily won over the inhabitants of the big town, and we were proud to think that of all the villages in the 'outlying' suburbs, ours had been chosen for the installation of the first public

29

fountain. That is why I adopted this superior tone to remind Agatha that we no longer needed rainwater to live, since in all weathers, from one end of the year to the other, we had at our disposal a fountain with a generous tap.

3

Late in the night, the rain at last stopped.

It stopped suddenly, when the earth wasn't expecting it. The angels of heaven had received the order to put down their water buckets immediately. They had undoubtedly received the order. Now they were looking at the black world of men, with an air of profound pity. And the hell at the centre of the earth, where the sinner damned for eternity dies of thirst, this hell at the centre of the earth began slowly to absorb the dirty water rejected by the heavens.

When you come to die, one day, do not follow, after your last breath, the beautiful, wide, shining road which Satan has constructed to deceive souls and entice them to his kingdom of darkness. Down there people drink only the rain water, which the earth itself rejects. When you leave for the other world, follow the humble and peaceful and unostentatious path which will lead your soul to salvation.

I was stretched out on my bamboo bed, a long time after Agatha's departure, and my imagination was playing with ideas of heaven and hell. 'People who have no public fountain on this earth, and who wait for the rain to get water which they call clean, are unfortunate,' I told myself: 'for they already drink in this world the same water that they will find later on in hell.' Fortunately, I believe that few people will go to hell. Basically, it is so difficult to go there: from childhood, our people have learned to beware of "the beautiful, wide, shining road which Satan has constructed to deceive souls and entice them to his kingdom of darkness". If there is still an individual among us who doesn't remember this important warning, I wonder what he can be like. No, nobody from our village will go to hell. Nobody, not even Eya, who is suspected of so many 'secret murders' – those which are carried out secretly in the invisible world of sorcery, and which cause the death of a man or a woman, whose soul becomes thereafter an eternal prisoner in the service of the magician – nobody, not even Mother Evil-Eye, that evil witch who prevents women from conceiving, not even Dina, who wants to show off to everybody and whose only strength is the unspeakable words which come from her devilish mouth . . .

Dina . . . what did she do to Endalé that morning? I wanted to tell you just now, but Agatha interrupted me.

Endalé arrived at the public fountain with an enormous receptacle in white enamel, which she set down without a by-your-leave on Mother Evil-Eye's bucket. There are women like that; they need only to have started the day on the wrong foot for them to imagine that they can draw water when it's not yet their turn. But, although one might have expected her to do so, it was not Mother Evil-Eye herself who intervened. She merely showed her surprise by clapping her hands, twice, in the manner of our women. It was Dina who let loose:

'Endalé, what are you doing there? Can't you wait till . . .'

'Wait, wait for what? Tell me: this water's for everybody, isn't it? Wait, wait . . . instead of getting water for your husbands, you spend your time gossiping like idiots, and you tell me to wait . . .'

'He, he, he,' shouted Dina, 'look at her, coming looking for trouble with her dirty bowl . . .'

'Dirty, yourself,' replied Endalé, keeping her bowl under the impassive tap. 'You say my bowl is dirty? Do you think it's as dirty as your face! Look at her, insulting my bowl . . .'

'Take it away, take it away immediately, or you'll see.'

'See what? I won't take it away . . . see what? You tell me.'

'I'll tell you right away. Come and see, let's leave the spout, just for a moment, we're going to see a little battle between two women who think they're tough. Come over here.'

Our women have no idea of joining forces in defence. Instead of uniting to oppose Endalé's impudence, they bravely decide that the affair going on before their eyes is no concern of theirs. Immediately they form a circle round the two women. Free entertainment for all.

'Since you're a woman of this village too,' repeated Dina (to remind everybody that she herself was a woman of our village, a fact of which we were only too well aware, believe me) 'then come into the street and show everybody what you're worth.'

'I won't come,' said Endalé. 'I won't come. My husband is waiting for me, he needs this water; I'm not like you, a wife who doesn't care.'

At this the other women began to boo Endalé, and to tell her that they hadn't realized that there was a creature as feeble as she was in our village. They all made fun of Endalé, but she went on drawing water without bothering about their mocking laughter. Then, her bowl filled, Endalé placed it on her head and prepared to depart. But at the very moment when she was leaving, the last-minute disaster, naturally happened: Dina gently tripped her and Endalé found herself on the ground, her bowl of water upset and her dress completely soaked. What an unexpected shower-bath . . . That was not all. Dina immediately jumped on her and began raining blows on her, saying that she had no right to carry pride to the extent of drawing water when it was not her turn in the queue. There was no reason, just because Endalé had a husband who occasionally worked in the town, for her to imagine herself the queen of our village. In any case, what was so wonderful about a husband who worked in the town? Did that make him better than other men? And anyhow nobody had ever yet discovered what kind of job this famous husband had in the town, and he didn't go there regularly . . . And what about Dina's husband, wasn't he a man too? Hadn't he bought her an umbrella of a kind that nobody would ever again find in the shops, because it was the only one of its kind in the world? (As if our village had ever wanted to own another umbrella like it . . .)

The other women were shouting, encouraging Dina to hit harder, and exhorting Endalé to stand up for herself a bit more. She tried to stand up for herself, to defend herself, and that was the beginning of the end: Dina really enjoyed tearing her dress, and then attacked unmentionable under-garments. When Endalé finally managed to get up, she presented a spectacle of nudity that was to say the least, unusual in our village. What an affair . . . And it was Mother Evil-Eye who lent her a little cloth to preserve her modesty. The news spread throughout Douala; indeed I am surprised that it didn't reach your ears.

But the next day, when tempers had cooled, Dina went to see Endalé and offered her friendship and apologies in the shape of ripe mangoes. But nothing, alas, could wipe out the everlasting shame of Endalé that morning when she had gone, like a good wife, to fetch water for her husband, from the public fountain in our village.

'No . . . ' Agatha Moudio had said, 'we don't need that kind of appliance which sows discord among us . . .'

It is true that our village could very well have done without that morning rumpus.

I went to sleep and dreamed of deep-sea fishing.

When I awoke, the next morning, I found my veranda bathed in sunlight, as if it had not rained for months. What weather, I thought. It pours with rain today, and tomorrow it's once again a brilliant summer's day. And yet, how it had rained the day before . . .

I saw Maa Médi coming back from the water-kiosk.

'Good morning,' I shouted to her, 'is everything fine with you this morning? How are you, Maa?'

Her way of answering that everything was fine and that she was very well was odd. I had an unpleasant feeling that my mother didn't love me very much that morning. You know how she is: one of those people who make no effort to hide their feelings, and who, with a gesture, or a single word, can convey to you that things are not what they should be. And on that particular morning things were not as Maa Médi would have wished, and with good reason: at the fountain, Mother Evil-Eye was busy telling everybody who would listen all that she knew of the latest events in the village; and naturally, on the front page of her spoken morning paper, there was the scandalous visit paid me the day before by Agatha, with the calm assurance that nobody had seen her. When I told you that Mother Evil-Eye, that vile witch, had eyes everywhere . . . so Maa Médi was furious with me, which is quite understandable after the advice she had previously given me about Agatha, the problem child of the region.

When my mother called me for breakfast that morning, I was far from feeling like giving myself airs. I made myself as small as possible and, bending in the usual way, I went into her house by the low door. The breakfast was good. It had the taste which it had always had for me since my childhood, and which instinctively made me stay with my mother as long as possible. While I ate I listened to the good woman. There could be no unclarified situation between her and me. I was her son, the only real gift she had ever received from heaven, the only person, today, that she could count on. I meant everything to her and I must not disappoint her. So why had I arranged a meeting with Agatha at my house, almost under the eyes of my mother, when it had been agreed that I would have nothing to do with the girl? In my house, almost under the eyes of my mother, as if I were scorning her and her advice? Why had I done that? Had I done it on purpose, to let her know that, in spite of her, my mother, I was going to marry this bad girl?

I took care to explain to Maa Médi, gently, that Agatha had come to my house without warning, and above all, without there ever having been any understanding between us that she would come to see me.

'Besides, you saw,' I said to my mother, 'for fear of being caught by you or anyone else, you saw how very well she managed to make it rain.'

'And what rain, good Lord, what rain,' added Maa Médi, more and more reassured by my explanations. 'I tell you that that kind of girl would do anything to get you. You must be very careful, son. You know you have a fiancée whom your dying father left you. The dead aren't allowed to open their eyes, otherwise . . .'

At this, my mother crossed the first and second fingers of her left hand. An indecent act on my part would re-open the eyes of my father sleeping in his grave, and would trouble the peace of his eternal rest. And what use is a corpse with its eyes open, since the rest of the body remains the prisoner of death, and total resurrection is not allowed? No, I had not the right to bring such terrible suffering on my father. I would not do so and, in any case, Maa Médi's fingers had just averted the danger.

I spent another week in the village, getting ready to leave for the fishing. The big fishing season was about to start. All over the village crews were at work, mending nets, and adding weights to the cast-nets. Whole hanks of black and white thread of all thicknesses were threaded in the shuttles of hard wood. The shuttles went swiftly to and fro through the stitches and made new stitches. The net grew bigger and bigger, accompanied by the songs and whistling of the workers. Other men were dealing with the provisions: we were to be away for a month; a month during which we should need adequate food to have the strength to face the huge waves of the rough sea . . . Everybody was making feverish preparations.

Then the morning for our departure arrived.

Our crew comprised six men, all tough types with a good knowledge of the harsh but fascinating task which awaited them. 'The high seas, I know them; of course I know them: I've been out hundreds of times, since I was a child,' each one of us would say. And it was true, we all knew them very well, with their big fish, and their little fish, and the hideous sharks, and the apocalyptic storms, and the comradeship between all the men of goodwill who sailed them, regardless of danger.

We gradually moved away from the river-bank of our village, dipping our paddles slowly into the calm water of the river. About three hours later we had reached the mouth, an estuary several kilometres wide. Here the difficulties would begin. Before us, the vast endless stretch of salt water demonstrated, in a way difficult to describe, the insignificance of man. The sea, calm at this moment, was covered with the silver grey of the cloudy sky. It was never blue at this point, at any time of year. In any case, the colour of the waves mattered little to us; what did matter was that these waves contained fish: a grey or blue sea is important only if it contains plenty of fish. And this sea had fish for all the inhabitants of Douala, and to spare. The heavens – not that part of the universe which offers itself graciously to our daily view – the real heavens, the invisible heavens of the other world, had given us a terrible sea with fish of all sorts. I was deep in these thoughts which, given the time and place, were highly irrelevant, when my cousin Ekéké, who was in our crew, suddenly asked:

'It's true, then, *La Loi*, what I heard this morning?'

'What did you hear?'

'Oh yes, tell us that you don't know, when it concerns you from start to finish; the women were talking about it this morning at the fountain; if you don't tell us the truth yourself, who *do* you expect to tell us? Were you hoping to give us a surprise? Ah, well, it's no good, for I tell you the women were talking about it this morning at the fountain . . . it's an open secret.'

'But, tell me: what are you talking about?'

'What? what? . . .' repeated the others, howling with laughter. For a moment they let their paddles fall into the water and float freely a few metres from the canoe. And they laughed . . . I rowed energetically towards the paddles, gathered them together, picked them up and hauled them back into the boat. I couldn't understand what they were talking about, nor why they were laughing, but the worst was that *they* were convinced that I was playing the innocent about a piece of news which 'concerned me closely'. I insisted, begging my companions to tell me what it was all about. I put on the serious expression I kept for important occasions, and then they understood that I was not joking. And believe me, I was truly astonished when I finally learned what was coming to me:

'What the women were saying at the fountain, this morning,' revealed Ekéké, 'what they were saying was that you are going to get married as soon as we get back from fishing.'

'Get married? That would be a fine thing, as soon as we get back from fishing. And who to then?'

'Oh, certainly not to Agatha Moudio,' replied my cousin.

And the others burst out laughing, so long and so continuously that in the end it got on my nerves.

'If you don't want to tell me what you've heard, that's your affair; you have a perfect right to hide whatever you want to hide from me. But I assure you there will be trouble if you keep on laughing at me like that. After all, if I'm to get married, I don't see what's so funny about it, even if I myself am completely in the dark about my own affairs.'

'That's just what's amusing us, that you are in the dark yourself, when the news is going round the whole village,' they said.

'Do you want to know?' asked Ekéké. 'I'll tell you; but mark my words, it's only because it's you, otherwise I wouldn't say a word. Listen carefully: you are going to marry, in a month . . . hm! hm! . . . oh, this cough I've had it for two days now, (the liar, he hadn't had a cough for two days; it was just to kill me with impatience) My brother, you are going to marry a girl, a pretty girl, yes, pretty it's true, but all the same rather a child, between ourselves. Couldn't you have waited for her to grow up a bit, don't you think?'

Naturally, I understood straight away: he meant Fanny, Tanga's daughter; but my cousin, who wasn't in the know about my father's will, didn't know that this girl had been intended for me long before her father had chosen the wife who would bear her. So, to Ekéké, the matter was quite new. My four other companions had also not known of it, until this morning when the information had become . . . official, at the village fountain. So you can understand their reaction on hearing the news: Fanny was still too young to be married. Had not I too had the same reaction during my conversation with Maa Médi?

We went on talking about all this for a long time on board, while each man, having taken up his paddle again, was rowing in the grey, still, calm water of the Wouri estuary. Then I had the idea of finding out if anything else had been said that morning about my approaching marriage.

'Nothing else,' replied Mbaka-the-less.

He was called this to distinguish him from Chief Mbaka, called Mbaka the Great, or simply Mbaka.

'Nothing else,' replied Mbaka-the-less. 'But when my wife told me this morning all that we have just been talking about, she succeeded in putting her finger on the root of the whole matter. Ah, brother Law, you're a deep one. We have been your brothers and companions for years and you tell us nothing: how do you expect us to help you find a wife if you keep secrets from us? If you yourself don't ask us to help you?'

Something else that I knew nothing at all about. I tried to make them believe that once again I didn't understand what they were talking about, but in vain. They begged me to believe that they would keep the secret about what was going to happen and what we were going to do. For this time it really was a secret, which hadn't even been mentioned at the fountain, although everything that happened, past, present and future, in our village, was usually advertised there every morning.

'And so you won't let me into the secret?' I asked without much hope.

'No, out of the question to tell you anything at all; but it's a promise, we'll help you when the time comes,' they replied.

4

We returned from the fishing-grounds, a month later, the boat full of smoked fish. I had just spent four unbearable weeks, asking myself the whole time what was awaiting me on my return to the village. As soon as I set foot on shore, I ran to Maa Médi's.

'I don't understand what's happening,' I told her. 'What plan has been made to get me married? And why wasn't I told anything about it? Explain, tell me everything, immediately, for the others refused to "divulge the secret" – as if the matter concerned anybody else but me . . .'

'Nothing serious is happening, son. Be calm. All you have to do is to obey your fathers, the elders of the village, you know that. Even if your poor father were still alive, he would tell you the same thing: you can't disobey them. All you need is to follow the advice they will give you.'

Maa Médi had a calm and serious manner which was far from usual with her. If you had seen her . . . she spoke like wisdom personified. And *I* still didn't know what to expect. I insisted, asking more and more questions. At last she spoke:

'I won't conceal from you, son, that since the other day, your future has caused me a lot of worry, you understand me: since the day when I found out that that abandoned girl was chasing you . . .'

'But, Maa, I had given you every reassurance on that question, at least I thought that . . .'

'Yes, I know, I know. You had convinced me that there was no danger from that quarter. But, my child, I know life better than you. Today you are big and strong and handsome and brave, but it is I who made you. I know what a woman can do to a man when she's determined to have him. Now Agatha is mad about you, otherwise she wouldn't come of her own accord and shut herself up with you on a rainy day, as she did the other day.'

My mother drew her bench nearer to mine, and spoke in a low voice:

'So,' she told me, 'I went to see Mbaka.'

'The Chief, or the less?'

'The Chief, of course; why would you expect me to go and see Mbaka-the-less? He may be married but that doesn't make him any more intelligent. What advice do you expect him to be able to give me, when he can't even keep his own wife as he should?'

Now you will remember that it was Mbaka-the-less who had revealed to me that a secret plan had been made for my marriage. So I still didn't understand a thing, for if it was a secret only the elders should have known about it. Punch must certainly have lived here once, I told myself. But listen rather to Maa Médi:

'I told him you wanted to get married. I didn't hide from him my anxiety about Agatha, and I reminded him that Tanga's daughter was intended for you. He quite understood the whole business. He thought about it, then he called the elders together. They were all there: Moudiki, Bilé, Ekoko, Mpondo-the-two-ends, king Solomon and even Eya. With Mbaka himself, that made seven of them. You hear me, son, the seven oldest men in the village met together to consider your case. That is why I beg you once again to do what they tell you, when the time comes. Don't fail to show them respect.'

'Very well, Mother, I understand. But what have they decided about me?'

'You will find out this very day. For it is agreed that, as

soon as you return, Chief Mbaka will summon you to talk to you about all this. You know it's not up to me to discuss with you what the men have decided to do, that's not my business; and even if I wanted to say anything I should find it difficult, since I know nothing at all about their final decisions.'

For once, I felt almost in despair. I had so hoped to know everything as soon as I got back, by talking to my mother, that I was rather shaken to hear her say that she herself didn't know what the elders had decided about me. Fortunately, Chief Mbaka didn't waste any time in sending for me.

When I got there, I found him seated among the others. All the elders were there: Moudiki, Bilé, Ekoko, Mpondo-the-two-ends, king Solomon, and even Eya. With Chief Mbaka, that made seven of them . . . seven elders of the village to discuss my case with me. I confess that their expression and their attitude didn't fail to impress me deeply.

The seven black faces assumed the expression kept for important occasions, reinforced by the semi-darkness of the room where the meeting was being held. They made me sit in the middle of the group and they spoke to me. As was right and proper, it was the Chief himself who spoke first.

'Listen, son,' he said, 'first I must warn you that the spirit of your father is present here, with us, at this very moment. Therefore know that we do nothing against his wishes. In any case, even if he were still alive, he would leave it to us, for he had confidence in the elders and great respect for them . . .'

Mbaka hesitated a moment, then continued:

'We are going to arrange your marriage. It is our duty, as it has always been the duty of the community to arrange marriages for its children. But if, following the example of some young people today, you think that you can sort out the question of your own marriage satisfactorily by yourself, we are ready to leave you a free hand, and not to concern ourselves with you any more in the matter. The only thing we have to ask you, is whether you consent to your marriage being arranged by the elders of the village, or whether, on the contrary, you consider it to be entirely your own affair, with which we should be wrong to concern ourselves. Answer us, son, don't be afraid, answer honestly: you are free to choose your own way.'

I understood: I was at the parting of the ways, the old and the new. I was absolutely free to choose what I wanted to do, or to allow to be done. Free only in theory, however, for the elders knew that I could not choose to dispense with their advice unless I decided *ipso facto* to go and live else-where, away from this village where everything worked according to age-old customs, in spite of the arrival of another form of civilization, which had manifested itself in particular by the installation of the public-fountain you already know about. And then, how could I dare to tell these grave and determined people that I wished to dispense with their advice? I tell you that there was there, among others, Eya, the terrible sorcerer, the husband of Mother Evil-Eye. To tell all those present that I refused their good offices amounted almost certainly to signing my death warrant. Everybody in our village lived in terrible awe of Eya, this man with eyes as red as ripe peppers, who, it was said, had already caused the disappearance of a certain number of people. And in spite of my strength, which was little by little taking its place in the legend of Douala wrestlers, I too was afraid of Eya. He was there, looking at me with an expression which he was trying to make both indifferent and paternal. His little eyes shone in the depths of hollow orbits, matching his thin cheeks. He can't have had much to eat when he was young. He was there, before me, a positive spectre of death, dressed in an immense cloth and a shirt of mildewed poplin. I dared not look at him directly. I thought, in my heart of hearts, that of all these men grouped round me only king Solomon could inspire me with a certain confidence. He, at least, was an honest man. Apart from the time when he genuinely wanted to make up stories – which, moreover, he was very good at – apart from those times, he said what he thought, with grains of wisdom worthy of the famous name he bore. It was, in any case, on account of this wisdom that our village had crowned him king, although throughout his life Solomon had never been anything but a stonemason. I turned my eyes towards him, as if to ask for advice. He nodded his head, lightly enough for the others not to see, but enough for me to understand. Yes, king Solomon shared the opinion of the group, and I had to accept this opinion, the opinion of all of them.

'Chief Mbaka, and you, my fathers,' I said, 'I cannot disobey you. I am a child of this village and I will follow tradition to the end. I declare before you that I leave to your experience and your wisdom the care of guiding me in life, until the distant day when I shall myself be called to guide others of our children.'

Each of the men showed his satisfaction in his own way, some coughing, some smiling, some taking another pinch of snuff.

'That is well, son,' said Chief Mbaka. 'That is the reply which we expected from our most worthy son, and we thank you for the confidence which you have willingly shown. Now, you may know all: tomorrow, we shall go and "knock on the door" of Tanga, for his daughter, Fanny . . . Spirit, you who see and hear us, do you hear what I say? I repeat that tomorrow we shall go and knock on Tanga's door, to ask his daughter's hand for our son, *La Loi*, as you yourself ordained before you left us. If you are not in agreement with us, show yourself in some way, and we will immediately change our plans . . .'

He spoke in this way to the spirit of my father, who was

44

present in the room, and we waited a few seconds for a possible manifestation. It did not come; nothing moved in the room, neither the door, nor the single window with its scanty light, which was covered by a little rectangular mat of woven raffia; we heard nothing, not even a step on the freshly beaten earth of the floor. Nothing: my father was giving us a free hand.

Then, the elders, in turn, explained to me what was to be done. The meeting lasted a good three hours, during which I was informed of the whole plan of action that they had carefully drawn up, and during which I also received so much advice that it will be difficult for me ever to remember it all. When I came out I knew that I was soon to be married, but that it would not be immediately, as my cousin Ekéké had claimed, no doubt to frighten me a bit. I went back, down to the riverbank, where my companions had stayed to sell some of the fish we had brought back, the greater part being intended for the big market at Douala, where we would go the next day. We only went back up to the village at nightfall. I went to Maa Médi's for dinner, and when I had finished I made haste to bid her goodnight. But instead of going to bed, I waited a while, and then went to see . . . Agatha Moudio.

Only the darkness made it possible for me to go to see her. When I reached her village I remained at some distance from her house, and twice whistled a tune which we had made up together, and which served as a signal whenever one of us wanted to see the other under cover of darkness. I had only to wait a few minutes. Agatha came out of her house by some door or other and came to join me. Only the dark night made such a meeting possible.

The next day, the elders of our village went to Tanga's, to 'knock on his door'. The operation consists of a courtesy call, for which one takes a bottle of spirits, 'real spirits' they call it, to make it clear that they mean whisky, or brandy, or at least rum, although this last is considered definitely inferior to the two first mentioned. One knocks at the door, one goes in, and one talks of this and that with the master of the house: the season is good, the rains will soon return, the women are doing their work in the fields, in spite of the oppressive heat, the children are good . . . One talks of everything, and only at the end, when the repertory of subjects of conversation is exhausted, then, one touches, as though by chance, on the main subject:

'Hm,' said king Solomon on that day, pouring himself a little whisky; 'hm, tell us, Tanga, do you remember the last words of your friend Edimo?'

'Edimo, the late Edimo, the father of Mbenda?'

'Yes, certainly, the very one; you have no other friends called Edimo that I know of?'

'No, that's true,' said Tanga.

And he swallowed a mouthful. This alcohol drunk neat livens you up quickly. So when Tanga began to talk about his memories of my father, his friend, who died before his eyes, it was mainly to recall the extraordinary times they had gone through together, when they were fishermen, long ago.

'If *I* can't remember Edimo, who else are you going to ask to tell you about him? Together we visited all the fishing villages on the Wouri estuary, and you ask me if I remember him? Wait, I'll tell you . . .'

'I know, I'm sure you haven't forgotten him,' said king Solomon. 'But what I'm asking you is to tell us if you remember his last words to you, before he closed his eyes for ever. Do you remember?'

'What? About his son? Of course I remember. He asked me to give my first daughter in marriage to his son. What do you think then? That I am not prepared to honour his memory? Do you know Fanny?'

'We know she exists and that she is your eldest daughter,

46

but we don't *know* her . . . we have never yet seen her. Do show her to us.'

King Solomon was the spokesman with Tanga. It was he whom the other elders had chosen to arrange this business of my marriage, and I was very pleased. I liked king Solomon very much.

Tanga didn't waste time answering. He got up promptly, went to the door, and shouted in the compound:

'Fanny, Fanny . . . Fanny . . .'

'Papa-a-a,' replied the distant voice of a little girl

'Come, Fanny, come and say hello to your fathers here.'

And the little girl, timidly, came and said hello to these hale and hearty old men, their eyes sparkling with Scotch whisky.

'Oh, Tanga, we had heard that you had a little daughter, but my impression is rather that she is already a woman,' said king Solomon, admiring the precocious child Fanny. In fact she looked more like a grown girl than a child of thirteen or fourteen.

When she had finished greeting everybody, she heard her father's order.

'You may go now.'

And she went. Just as she was crossing the threshold, relieved to get back into the fresh air, her father called her back:

'Listen,' he said, 'go to your uncle Njiba's. Tell him I need to see him immediately.'

Fanny ran to her uncle Njiba's. He arrived almost at once. He found the bottle of whisky half empty, but he nevertheless expressed his pleasure that there was still some left:

'Blessed be thou, oh bottle, come by ship from a distant land. My eyes have never seen your country, but my tongue knows the exquisite savour of the liquid you contain. Blessed be thou, oh bottle manufactured by the whites.'

Then he immediately protested:

'What's this, Tanga, you have a thing like this in your house, and you call me only when it's already finished?'

'Njiba,' Tanga then cried, 'you should begin by saying good day to the strangers you find in my house, instead of going in for drunken protests. What will they think now?'

'My brothers,' said Njiba, whose eyes were becoming used to the strange light in the room, 'my brothers, don't be annoyed that I didn't greet you when I came in. As soon as I saw this bottle on the table, it fascinated me so much, that I had eyes only for it, and nothing else. My brothers, forgive me, forgive me. May Nyambé the Almighty keep you, and make you happy under this roof, which is that of my full brother.'

The others also made polite noises. Then Tanga quickly explained to his brother what had brought these men from our village. Naturally, Njiba would only have lent half an ear to this tale if Tanga had not first poured him a whole glass of whisky.

'Brother Njiba, if I drink, you must drink too; because I am you and you are me. What is mine is yours and what is yours is mine. Drink.'

Njiba swallowed a large mouthful, then, without putting down his glass, he once again filled his cheeks with whisky, swilled his mouth carefully, savoured the liquid for an instant, and, finally, swallowed this second mouthful.

'Ah-h-h,' he said, 'believe me, there's nothing like it for rheumatics, those "snakes of the night" who no longer leave you in peace as soon as old age creeps on.'

He looked at what was still left in his glass, handed it to his brother for a refill, got it and put the glass down near him on the table, complaining:

'I've already told you several times to buy some proper glasses. You're killing us with these little toys. They're like

48

dolls' glasses . . . you're killing us with thirst, Tanga, killing us.'

'It's true,' said Moudiki, 'it's true that the French don't know how to make these things. In German times, we had glasses, real glasses worthy of the name . . . Oh, don't talk about that any more, it reminds me of so many extraordinary things. I can't even tell you all about it now: glasses . . . big beer glasses, like that . . . Father had some of all kinds, in German times. I wonder why those people left. Perhaps they didn't like our country much.'

'Me too, I think they didn't like our country, although we are told lies here and told they had to leave because they had lost the war,' said Bilé.

'Lost the war? How could the Germans have lost the war? Is it possible? And who in the world could possibly have made them lose it? These softies who are here now? Come on now . . . tell me something else.'

Our men were like that. For them, regret for the German times was such that they were always ready to compare the present and the past, and always, naturally, to the advantage of the past. Today, however, this was not the question. These men, gathered in an African house, drinking Scotch whisky out of French glasses while they remembered Germany's former greatness, these men had undertaken to lay down the main lines of my future estate as a married man.

'You drink, brother Njiba,' said Tanga suddenly, 'you drink, and you don't even bother to find out what it is you're drinking to . . .'

'That's just what I was going to ask you: you simply got in first. Tell me then: what must I pay for the pleasure of drinking this excellent alcohol of the whites?'

'Nothing at all. You're not being asked to spend a cent, even if you are very rich. But look at the brothers who have come to see us. Just now they asked me a question, which it's

49

your job to answer; listen carefully. They asked me if I remembered the last words of my friend Edimo, about my daughter Fanny, who, as you know, was not yet born at that time . . . And what is your answer to that?'

Njiba swallowed another mouthful, coughed and took his time before replying:

'What do I say? What I am going to say? Well, you, my brother, you're a cool customer, that's what I have to say first. Some men come to see you one morning, they give you a drop of whisky to drink, and you immediately prepare to give them your daughter . . . and you arrange for me to be the person who says yes, so that "the others" in the village, can say tomorrow that it was I who gave Fanny away without informing them . . . and you ask me what my answer is?'

Our people looked at each other. Bilé took another pinch of snuff and sneezed three times. There was still some whisky in the glasses; each one sought in it the strength necessary to pursue the negotiations. In any case, the turn events had taken was not unexpected. What would have been surprising would have been to see Tanga, or his brother Njiba, allow the visitors to return home with the certainty that Fanny was officially theirs. These things don't happen so quickly. Njiba's reply was therefore not particularly disturbing. Tanga confirmed this, by adding:

'You understand what my brother Njiba means. You came to knock on my door. I must now go and inform "the others" of your visit. Only they can decide on the outcome of your request. I personally can't tell you anything until I have consulted them. I merely undertake to keep you informed of the answer they give me . . . but' – he hesitated a moment – 'I mean if you have anything to send them, so that I don't go to them empty-handed, it would make things much easier.'

Our people had, naturally, foreseen all this. King Solomon opened a bag which he had kept beside him since arrival at Tanga's and took out . . . a second bottle of Scotch whisky, of the famous Johnny Walker brand.

'The chap walking on this,' said king Solomon, pointing to the picture on the label of the square bottle, 'the white walking there has only to go and speak to your people on our behalf. Let him speak well, and *you*, you will let me know when and how we can come and claim our bride.'

Everybody laughed at this joke of the king's; they emptied the first bottle and the glasses and then separated. When I got back in the evening from the market in the town, where I had been with my mates to sell fish, I went to king Solomon's to find out what they had said and done at Tanga's.

'My son,' he said, 'everything is going as it should. You can't expect your wife at your house tomorrow, but I can assure that it's now only a question of time. Time will arrange things properly . . .'

I left reassured and praying that time would take its time. As long as it was a question of Fanny I was in no hurry, and I was still hoping that, given time, my mother would manage to change her mind about Agatha Moudio, and that in the end it would be she whom I married first, before facing my inevitable marriage with Tanga's daughter. In any case, the visit to Tanga, as related to me by king Solomon, led me to think – faint ray of hope – that Fanny's family might equally well refuse our offer of marriage. After all, nothing obliged them to accept: the last wishes of a man who was not one of them could hardly be binding on their whole community. 'Lord,' I said to myself, 'if they could just have the bright idea of refusing, or of making things so complicated for us that we are obliged to give up ourselves . . .'

I went to Maa Médi's for dinner. I told her in detail about my day at the big market in the town. I counted out in front of her all the money I had earned.

'This,' I told her, giving her a share of it, 'this is for you This other share is for you to keep safely for me.'

My mother was the best banker in the world, and I was flattering her hugely by showing my trust in her in this way. So many children, nowadays, were leaving their mothers as soon as they could earn their own living . . . I also took a bit of pocket-money. And after dinner, I did the same as the day before. I met Agatha Moudio in the same way. I gave her a pretty dress and a multi-coloured scarf which I had bought for her at the market, after the receipts had been shared between me and my mates. Agatha adored pretty dresses and I knew it. There are people who smile whenever I tell them that I bought a dress for Agatha. 'How did you manage about trying it on?' they ask me. Well, I didn't try it at all, and I explained as much to the young lady:

'If it's too long for you, you can shorten it, and if it's too full, you need only take it in a bit at the waist.'

She was in the seventh heaven, and I was happy to see her so.

. . . A few days later, Tanga, the father of Fanny, sent a messenger to Chief Mbaka and informed him that he would like to meet some of our people. The next day, king Solomon and Bilé went to Deido.

'Look,' Tanga told them, 'I have the impression that luck was with you the other day. The white walking jauntily on the square bottle walked well for you. The people of my community are ready to meet you as soon as you like, to discuss this proposal seriously . . . in detail; and they have asked me to tell you so.'

The king thanked Tanga for this good news. When one is the sponsor in an affair like that, one likes to see progress being made, and especially progress in the right direction. A date was immediately fixed for a meeting at which, I supposed, they would negotiate Fanny's marriage.

A month later, the appointed day arrived.

They met again at the house of Njiba, who was Fanny's sponsor, just as king Solomon was mine. There was a big feast and wines of all kinds, from grey-white palm-wine drawn from brown calabashes to red wine brought from Europe in wicker demijohns. A good blow-out doesn't stop people talking . . . and they talked, and talked. There were remarks of all kinds, from the insignificant joke which nobody laughs at but the teller, to the hardly veiled insult, which from time to time casts considerable doubt on the favourable outcome of the negotiations.

'Our daughter,' said Njiba, 'our daughter is not the kind to be sold. If you wish, we will simply give her to you. I am saying give, and I know what I am saying . . . uncle, pour me a little more of this wine which the whites make for us. Pour me some, for I have something to say to our visitors . . .'

They poured him some. He got up, raising the glass to his lips:

'Yes,' he went on, 'I say that we will give you our daughter. Don't misinterpret my words; I am her uncle, that is her father, and I shall be the spokesman from start to finish. Let me have a drink . . . I repeat that you must not misinterpret what I say. In any case, you will have our daughter only if you accept my offer. You may take it or leave it. But I know you will accept, for it's an altogether exceptional marriage. Just think, your son was engaged to our daughter even before she was born. Take her, give us nothing. There, I have spoken, I have finished. If you have anything to say, I am listening.'

Njiba sat down and emptied his glass without missing a word of what the others were saying around him. Then it was king Solomon's turn to speak:

'Brother,' he said, 'we thank you for the generous offer which you have just made us. You have a good heart and it is particularly pleasing to us to know that this wife of our son comes from a family with such a generous disposition. You don't want us to pay anything. We will . . .'

'I tell you that our daughter is not for sale, like a goat,' interrupted Njiba. 'It is not our custom to do that here. If you want to buy a wife for your son, this is not the place to come to. We are not asking a penny from you, even if you have more money than you know what to do with.'

'We thank you,' continued the king. 'We thank you all the more, since we are far from considering ourselves rich. Moreover, we too are no longer at the primitive stage where men buy and sell women. So everything is fine, brothers, everything is fine, isn't that so?'

'You are right,' replied our people. 'You are right, everything is fine, since we have no money to buy the wife of our son, or for that matter any other woman in the world.'

This was not strictly true. They naturally had a little money for this kind of transaction, but the fact is that we had long since stopped calling it 'buying' or 'selling' a wife. We didn't even attribute a symbolic value to the giving of a little money when taking a wife. No, we were not what Europeans sometimes call civilized blacks, with a note of pride in their voice which indicates that the work of civilization undertaken by them throughout the world is beginning to bear fruit; we were simply practical people. We considered it necessary to compensate parents from whom we were taking a daughter, to make up as it were for the physical help provided by their daughter, which they were losing. This is what king Solomon explained to the people of Deido.

In fact, the decision of our hosts had somewhat surprised us. They, who were so fond of money that the fact was broadcast in dozens of popular songs, were now showing themselves generous towards us. It seemed suspicious to us, but king Solomon was a wily diplomat; he did not refer to this curious, and to say the least, unexpected point. He was content to follow up his idea in reply to Njiba, who was listening, his eyes red from wine.

'I say then that everything is fine. However, we always like what we do to be well done, and we like to see everybody satisfied when we have done something. Listen carefully: we don't want to buy Fanny, but, brother Njiba, I ask you to tell me in what way we could help her parents to feel that they have lost nothing by giving her to us for ever. That seems a good idea to me.'

Njiba called on one of his people to reply:

'Tobo,' he said, 'Tobo, will you say something in reply to what Solomon has just said? As for me. I get the distinct impression that he doesn't understand my language. Speak to him, will you.'

'Solomon,' said Tobo, 'getting up and holding with one hand his cloth, which had almost come off. 'Solomon, you know I can tell you nothing new. You have known me since we were children; do I tell lies? Tell me, am I a liar?'

'You are not a liar, Tobo, you do not tell lies,' replied the king.

'Then,' continued Tobo, 'I can tell you nothing new. But I must say that this business, which we here call "marriage", is something that the people of this tribe know better than you can imagine. Do you know that with our boys and girls, we celebrate several marriages a year in this village? No no, I'm not saying that to put you off, only to make you understand that Fanny is not the first girl from here who is leaving us to go and live elsewhere . . . her marriage will not be the last we have to deal with, either. So if my brother Njiba tells you to take the bride without paying anything in exchange, you mustn't be surprised. Simply take the woman, and take her away. Whatever you want to do apart from that, is your affair. If you want to make it rain tons of gold on the heads of Tanga and his wife, that is purely your affair; as for us, we ask for nothing. Nothing at all, not even a drink.'

'I repeat my thanks,' said king Solomon. 'Thank you for wishing to spare us so much expense. But you must know, brother, that we are also not dealing with the first marriage in our village. Now, up to now, we have never taken a bride completely free of charge. Never,' repeated the king, 'and if there is anybody here from our village who can remember an affair like today's let him say where, when and how we have ever taken a bride without putting our hands into our pockets . . .'

'Never,' replied Mbaka, the Chief, sitting heavily in his armchair. 'Never,' he insisted, 'and we are not prepared to accept such an offer.'

What Chief Mbaka said expressed what he thought, the more so because Njiba's proposition, confirmed by Tobo was beginning to seem to us more and more suspicious.

'Good,' said Njiba then, getting up, 'good, we will give you satisfaction. After all, you have taken the trouble to come all this way to see us, and we can't disappoint you. Since you insist on giving us something in exchange for Fanny, you will certainly be glad to know that the mother of our daughter desires a large chest containing dresses, headscarves, shoes, and pleasant-smelling perfume; that her father would like a big new cloth, a white poplin shirt and a top hat, and finally, that the people of this village would not look very kindly on the departure of their daughter unless you gave them something like a little cooking salt for the women, and a little tobacco for the men.'

'There we are,' said king Solomon, satisfied, 'now it begins to look like a real Douala marriage. Why couldn't you speak frankly? Between ourselves, we don't need to beat about the bush to tell each other what we think. So much for the presents. Now, shall we talk about the cash?'

'Nothing,' said Njiba, 'I tell you we are giving you our daughter for nothing . . .'

'Speak carefully, brother,' said the king. 'We want to pay something, no matter what, but . . .'

'Then, if you wish, you have only to give us a 500-franc note.'

The king uttered a sigh of relief. Everything seemed normal to us now: for the 500-franc note, which at that time had a fixed value, was the current amount for a bride-price. It was now clear to us that the people of Deido had made a lot of fine speeches for nothing and that their display of generosity was no doubt a hidden way of getting out of us even more money and 'presents' than were usually asked in similar cases. Fundamentally, they have always had this crude mentality of exploiters, and I am almost sure that if my father hadn't had one of them as a friend we shouldn't have come to ask for the hand of Fanny, either for me, or for any other child of our community who was looking for a wife. But, as you know, my marriage had been arranged a long time before, at a moment of final solemnity and it was our duty to do everything to carry out the last wishes of my father. Tanga and his people were also aware that we would do everything to carry out these wishes, and they were preparing, naturally, not to make things easy for us. They intended, no doubt, to make things terribly difficult for us, in spite of the attractive proposals that they had pretended to put forward at the beginning of the negotiations. You will see:

'All right, then, if you wish, you may give us a 500-franc note,' said Njiba.

He spoke with an air of indifference, as if he really didn't care whether or not he received the sum he was asking. King Solomon was going to say something, when somebody else, on Njiba's side, raised his voice:

'My brothers, Tanga, Njiba, and Tobo, you have no

57

right to treat us as you are doing at present: you call us to a meeting as important as this, and you explain to us only half of what is going on . . . You're now talking about Fanny's dowry, and you are confusing all kinds of things, so that I personally no longer understand a thing: the chest for the mother, the salt for the women, the tobacco, the money . . . Am I then to understand from this that the betrothal is already complete and that in fact what we are talking about today is Fanny's marriage? If so, I wish somebody would tell me when this betrothal took place, for I personally don't remember ever having heard about it . . . at least, not with the son of Edimo.'

Obviously, the man was not pleased. But wasn't it all part of an act carefully prepared in advance in order to make things as complicated as possible for us?

'I was coming to that,' said Njiba. 'Yes, Solomon, that is a point which we completely forgot to raise when you came to see us the other day. I will explain to you; you must understand. You know that Edimo, on the threshold of death, asked Tanga to give his first daughter in marriage to his son Mbenda, whom I see sitting over there. Now, when Tanga's third wife produced a daughter, long after Edimo's death, nobody from your side appeared to remind us that Fanny had come into the world for you people. And nobody came, either, during the years which followed. Now our daughter is at present almost fourteen. You can well imagine that in all that time she has not been without suitors . . . But that, as you must see, is your own fault, since you didn't show up. We did indeed expect you, but we couldn't come bothering you, for we should have lost face if you had said you were not interested in our daughter. Fortunately, when you at last raised the subject, some time ago, it was still not too late. Fanny's latest suitor is a young man from Bonapriso, called Manfred Essombé. He is a salesman with the Sudanese Company, and he has a good position; but naturally, we should certainly give preference to your son, in view of the exceptional nature of your approach to us.'

So here was something else: was Fanny already betrothed? Ah, I thought, if I had known sooner, I would have used it against the apparently unanswerable arguments of Maa Médi. But I was hearing the truth only now, when it was impossible to retreat. But let's hear the rest of Njiba's revelations, and perhaps all hope of getting rid of Fanny was still not lost to me? The man took an enormous swig of palm-wine. He switched easily from one kind of wine to another and it seemed to do him no harm.

'So, this being the case,' he went on, 'you see what we shall have to do if you insist on having our daughter Fanny . . . we shall have to break her engagement to this young man from Bonapriso who loves her, but oh, so much . . .'

'It's tiresome,' said Bilé, one of our men. 'It's tiresome, we understand that; but for us it's a question of carrying out the request of a man who was dear to us. And you all know here, that the son of Edimo, whom we wish to give as a husband to your daughter, is the strongest wrestler in Douala. We're not offering you just anything, just anybody; see for yourselves: get up, *La Loi*, so that they can see you properly.'

I got up and threw out my chest boldly.

'There,' said Bilé, 'there is the husband for Fanny. Tell me, Njiba, have you anybody better to offer to your daughter?'

I created the expected impression and Bilé sat down wearing a satisfied smile. I showed myself off for only a few seconds and sat down in my turn. When Njiba spoke again it was to say the last word on the affair and to announce the final decision:

'It's tiresome, indeed, as my brother Bilé has just said. It's really very tiresome,' insisted Njiba. 'For we here really wanted with all our heart to give you our daughter for nothing. But you see the kind of complications that are necessarily involved in a change of fiancé. The point is that this young man, of whom I was speaking a minute ago, has already done a lot for our family; presents of all kinds, money, and, to be honest, all that remained was to fix a date for him to come and claim his bride . . . If we suddenly broke off his engagement to Fanny, he would be perfectly entitled to ask us to repay all that he has already given us . . . you see what I mean: have you the resources to face such a possibility?'

We had already realized, for some minutes, what Njiba was getting at. You see . . . when I told you earlier that these people merely wanted to exploit all those who came asking for their daughter in marriage . . .

' . . . have you the resources?'

To answer that we first needed to know what might be the total of the amount to be repaid. However, the day we were living through, in front of people who must at all costs be made to consider us as important people, didn't leave us much time for bargaining. The king got up immediately, and, without even first inquiring how much we should be obliged to repay, declared:

'The resources, the resources . . . what do you think then? In spite of my age, I still work all day. As for our young people, there is not one who stays doing nothing in the village. So, to tell you that we are men of substance is, in other words, to say that even if this substance were insufficient at the present moment, we could work hard and increase it rapidly, if that were necessary. Speak, brother Njiba, tell us how much this young man from Bonapriso has given you altogether, and *I* shall repay you.'

Human pride. We were not, I admit, extremely poor; but all the same we needed to watch these greedy men who wanted to take advantage of us. We musn't let them think that we were about to fall into their trap. But too bad; it was king Solomon, my sponsor, who was our spokesman with them, and what he had just said reflected all our thoughts. In any case, none of us would have contradicted him, for fear of making ourselves appear incapable of financing a proper betrothal.'

'I am afraid of disappointing you,' said Njiba, wiping his brow with a brand-new white handkerchief. 'Yes, I am very much afraid, but facts are facts. You musn't think that we're trying to overcharge you. I tell you that our present intended son-in-law, this young man from Bonapriso is a man with a very good position with the Sudanese Company. So, when I tell you how much you will have to repay us on his account, don't start exclaiming that I've asked more than was necessary . . .'

'Speak, go on, speak,' said Chief Mbaka impatiently.

'Very well,' said Njiba, 'if you really want Fanny, you will have to pay something like seven thousand francs . . .'

'What?' asked Tobo, 'you say seven thousand francs? I assume you're talking only about the cash? For you know that this child of Bonapriso has given us a lot more than that since . . .'

'Yes, that's right, I'm not mentioning the pans, nor the jewels and other things.'

'Seven thousand francs, said king Solomon, 'that's not too bad. But, tell me, if I understand you right, you are busy selling us your daughter without actually doing so?'

'Oh, no, Solomon, don't say such a thing,' replied Njiba. 'You mustn't say such a thing. What would people think of us if we were to sell you Fanny? We are not savages . . . and I hope you didn't mean to insult us by saying that. Only, as I pointed out just now, facts are facts. We are already doing you a favour: accepting your son rather than somebody from a distant village, who has, however, already done a lot to help our family materially. Believe me, we aren't trying to cheat you, for this money that you will give me I shall immediately give back to the young man who was here before you. I understand that you are anxious to fulfil the last wishes of one of your people; only, you will have to help us, in that case, to overcome our own difficulties, which in any case arise from the fact that you delayed getting in touch with us.'

'That's all right,' said king Solomon. 'We're going to help you. Just give us a few days to allow us to get together the money you want, and we will give you a son-in-law worthy of you.'

This last answer was welcomed on both sides by approving nods, or by murmurs, all of which signified: 'Indeed, there's no one like king Solomon to deal with a marriage settlement.'

There followed discussions on points of detail; then, towards nightfall, we separated. We had spent the whole day arguing with Tanga's people.

5

The truth of the matter was that Njiba and his people were surprised to find that we hadn't argued about the price that they were asking us to pay. Seven thousand francs ... a fortune at that time. Why the devil had king Solomon accepted that without demur? We had never yet paid so much to get a wife, and everyone was reminding himself of this.

'Don't worry yourselves, I have a plan in my head,' said the king, when, on the way home, we showed our anxiety and asked him where he expected to find all that money.

'Those people think we are imbeciles,' he said; 'and they think they are cunning. But we have more cunning foxes than they have, and that's what I'm going to try and show them. Wait . . .'

As soon as we got home we were once more assembled to hear the suggestions of the wise king.

'You, Ekéké,' he said, 'will go tomorrow to the Company. You will act very tactfully. You will try to discover, by any discreet means, if there really is a Manfred Essombé with them, if he is really engaged to Fanny, if things are going smoothly, and if it is true that the young man has given "them" so much money . . .'

. . . Beginning the next day, each one set about thinking over or carrying out the orders of king Solomon. It goes without saying that the most important was the inquiry, for which he had made my cousin Ekéké responsible. When Ekéké returned to the village in the evening, he informed us that a Manfred Essombé did in fact work as a salesman with the Sudanese Company and that he had been trying, for at least two years, to win Tanga's daughter. 'But these people, my cousin had been told in confidence, are the biggest rogues in Douala. This young man from Bonapriso gives them all his month's salary, and more . . . and up to now, they won't give him his bride. They have put off the date of the marriage at least ten times. One really wonders what they want.' Then Ekéké told us that Manfred had certainly given a lot of money to his 'in-laws', as well as numerous presents, but that it was impossible, seeing the chap's position, that the total could be seven thousand francs.

'That's exactly what I thought too,' said king Solomon.

'Now, let each of you give what he can, and we'll go and see Tanga . . .'

'Why Tanga? It's Njiba who's running the show.'

'Yes, that's so . . . quickly, give me all you can manage.'

Everybody went off to see what savings he had. Nobody had, a few days previously, imagined he was going to contribute money for my marriage . . . at least, not so soon. However, each one did so without protest, and willingly gave what he could. In this way, the king collected three thousand francs. With Chief Mbaka, Moudiki and me, he went to Njiba's.

We found him away from home. His wife gave us seats on the veranda, and there we awaited his return. 'He won't be long coming back,' said the woman. 'He told me he wasn't going very far . . .' Then she went back to her work.

It was a black day for the children: their mother was busy preparing for them the big dish of weekly laxative medicine. As soon as she had finished, she called them, shouting: 'Come in, come in all of you, the pancakes are ready.' Immediately a cloud descended on the veranda. There were nine of them, from the eldest, fifteen, to the youngest, two. Njiba's nine children came running in answer to their mother's shout. 'This morning,' she said when they were all there, 'I'm going to give you two things: first, the pancakes, but, before that, the purge.' The children's faces showed their disappointment: this 'purge' that they didn't like at all, what was it doing there, just before the pancakes? And then, there was their mother making it sound quite natural to drink the medicine 'first' before eating the pancakes. And then, every week, it was always the same thing: always this medicine at regular intervals. And it was green, green and sticky, and it smelled horrible, horrible. And they had to drink it, or they would be deprived not only of the golden pancakes which were waiting silently in a white enamel dish on the table, but also of the midday meal and the evening meal, and then their father would beat them for the slightest thing they did wrong throughout the day. It's no use refusing, thought the eldest, coming forward and saying, beating his chest: '*I*'m not afraid of that . . . I'll show you how to drink it.' He drank and made a face hardly likely to encourage the others. But it was over: now, he had a healthy tummy for a whole week. He was congratulated and he knew that, an hour later, he would be able to eat two pancakes. One by one, the other children also came to be cleansed. The sight reminded me of my own childhood, when Maa Médi used to inflict this 'purge' on me: an enormous glass filled with this famous green and sticky and foul-smelling liquid, an unmeasured dose, heavens . . . and Maa Médi's eternal 'that will clean out your tummy'. I looked at these children and I told myself it was fortunate that this torture for the sake of cleanliness didn't last one's whole life through.

Meanwhile Njiba arrived.

'Good morning,' king Solomon said to him. 'When one has a debt, one's mind doesn't rest. One must pay off this debt at all costs. So here I am. Take this purse and tell us when we may come back to claim our son's bride. Tell us today . . .'

The man smiled as he took the purse, which he weighed with a dubious expression and then put it on his knees.

'There are seven thousand francs here? You say there are seven thousand francs here?' he asked.

'Njiba,' replied king Solomon, 'I should really like to know: who do you take me for? For the white man who mints money? Seven thousand francs, do you think that's so easy to find? Do you think I've planted behind my house a tree which has bank notes for leaves and coins for seeds? Count the money, yourself, and see how much there is, and then fix the date of the marriage. This engagement's been going on for twenty years and we've already put in a lot of walking for our son's bride . . . the sun is too hot these days.'

Njiba patiently counted the coins and notes.

'Three thousand francs,' he said, 'that's not enough. How do you expect me to repay the rest?'

'What rest? Are you going to keep on telling me that this child of Bonapriso, who is only a salesman in a shop, could give you as much as seven thousand francs, when we couldn't, several of us together, raise such a sum? You know, Njiba, we're not children. Take this money. I know it's quite enough, I even suspect it's more than enough. Take it, and give us our bride.'

'Don't talk yet about "our bride", for "the others" still have to speak. If you like, I'll keep this money and discuss the question with them. If they agree, then I'll send you word to come and claim your son's bride . . .'

We chatted a little longer, then we left Njiba. As we were leaving his house, he called me back: 'Son,' he said to me, 'even if it doesn't occur to you to bring me something from time to time, it doesn't matter, although I must tell you that I won't refuse your presents. But if you want everything to go well, don't forget to go now and then and visit the mother of your future wife. That often helps a lot.'

I understood what that meant: Njiba and his people were not interested in letting Fanny go immediately. For them, the engagement was just beginning, for an indefinite period, although Maa Médi on the other hand was trying to get me married as soon as possible in order to escape from Agatha Moudio. But I tell you again, king Solomon had his plan, and he was proposing to put it into operation at a favourable moment. We went home and the days passed. When they pass, they can't be recalled, as you will see later.

For Agatha, this time during which I no longer visited her

was too long. Naturally, the news of the steps we were taking with a view to my marriage had reached her. She no longer knew what attitude to take with me, since I hadn't spoken to her about all this, any more than I had said that I wouldn't marry her. But when she learned that I was in agreement with my people and that I was going to marry little Fanny, she could no longer contain her anger. One afternoon she arrived at my house like a whirlwind and poured out all the bitterness she felt against me. I was unfaithful, because I had let her hope I would marry her, and during this time, I was planning to marry another girl – an insignificant little miss – while she was kept waiting. And did I think it was impossible for her to find another man, even several men more interesting than myself, to replace me in her affections? And did I think she had thrown herself at my feet because nobody else wanted her? In her anger, she said so many things all at once, that I can remember only half of what I heard. Women are like that. When anger takes hold of them, they tell you a lot of things. They also break the crockery. And Agatha didn't go home until she had smashed before my eyes the three glasses and the five china plates which made up the whole of my bachelor household. I am sure that if I had owned other breakable things, she would not have deprived herself of the pleasure of robbing me of them all so that Fanny would find nothing at all in my house when she arrived . . . 'If she ever comes,' said Agatha. Her behaviour almost made me lose my temper, and I made superhuman efforts not to explode myself. I didn't want Maa Médi, when she returned from her plantation in the evening, to die of a heart-attack when she learned that this 'bad girl' had come and started a scandalous scene in our house, in broad daylight, for, to my mother, that would have suggested that, even quite recently, I had given Agatha the idea that I would marry her. In any case, at that moment I would have strongly denied that I would ever marry a woman like her, after all she had just done and said. But, as I tell you, when days pass, you can't recall them. Listen to the rest of my story.

Yes, on that day I did all I could to avoid a scandal, and above all to save Maa Médi from the unpleasant knowledge that the beautiful Agatha had been 'to see me'. But it was useless. She heard the news as soon as she got back from the fields, at the public fountain, where she had gone to get water for the evening meal. And for the rest of the evening I spent my time explaining to my mother that Agatha had acted completely on impulse, for there had never so far been any question of a promise of marriage between us. Maa Médi finally went to bed, once more mollified by my explanations. 'Her anxious nature,' I thought to myself, 'has at bottom more need of my support than I of hers. And yet, she insists on thinking that I'm still her little boy, her child whom it is her duty to protect. Oh, parents . . .'

Almost a month had gone by since we had given our money to Njiba, and yet he showed us no sign of life. We were beginning to get worried. I went now and then to Tanga's to see my fiancée and her mother. Each time I went there, I was accompanied by two or three young men from our village, and we went with our arms full of presents for the family. The engagement was taking a normal course. And yet, talking to Tanga, himself the father of my fiancée, I couldn't find out anything about the result of the negotiations for my marriage, for Njiba alone was responsible. Two months passed, during which I only went fishing for a few days, although it was already the season for deep-sea fishing. Finally, one evening, king Solomon went to see Moudiki and Chief Mbaka:

'That's enough now,' he told them. 'We must act. For just suppose for a moment that that drunkard Njiba hasn't even handed over the money to his people and that he's spending it on drink, that would mean we had lost everything, including the innumerable presents which our son is endlessly giving to Fanny's family.'

'That's impossible,' said Chief Mbaka. 'You know they've already broken off the engagement to the chap from Bonapriso. Since he's been going there, *La Loi* has never reported meeting the young fellow at Tanga's . . . not once since he's been going there . . . nor the friends who go with him. So, it's obvious: the other engagement is off, and for us, everything's in order. I don't know what's worrying you.'

'What worries me is the amount of time which has passed without our knowing where we are with those people. Personally, I mistrust them.'

'Yes,' said Moudiki, 'I think the king's right, Mbaka. Why the devil doesn't Njiba tell us what they've done with our money? It seems odd to me: we give the money, and we haven't got the bride, and we don't even know what has happened to the money itself . . . and they have the nerve to talk about a free marriage. I think we should act, Chief, and act at once.'

Moudiki lost confidence even in his brothers when it was a question of money. But he was right, this time: we had to act. King Solomon acquiesced with a nod, pleased to have support.

'Very well,' said Mbaka, at last. 'It's agreed, we shall act. Solomon, you have only to summon the young men that we've chosen, and tell them that it's tomorrow evening. Ask *La Loi* if he's going to see his fiancée tomorrow evening. If so, then "it" will be the next evening. If not, then do as we decided . . .'

The next evening, I had no intention of going to Tanga's. First, I had no money to spend on presents that day, and secondly, I wanted to go and see . . . yes, Agatha Moudio, whom I hadn't seen again since the day when she broke all my things. When I tell you that I loved her . . . two main reasons made me want to go and see her the next evening:

69

one, I had heard that she had gone back to leading a pretty disorderly life, pretty scandalous, said our people, who were again criticizing her long and inexplicable visits to the European quarter: and secondly, I was fed up with these visits to Tanga's, which I spent chatting to the friends who went with me, or with Fanny's parents, without ever having a chance to say a word to the girl herself. At that time, such was the rule: the fiancé said nothing, or almost nothing, to his bride-to-be, through the long evenings of these famous present-bearing visits. In any case, Fanny was still a little girl and I had not yet begun to think of her as a girl who was soon to become my wife. It was true that the confidence which Tanga and his wife showed in me increased daily, and latterly they had sometimes allowed their daughter to see us off at the end of our visit to a few yards from their house: but I couldn't pretend that this little companion, who was dumb with shyness, made my heart beat any faster.

'No,' I said to king Solomon, 'I'm not going to Tanga's tomorrow night, I'll go another day.'

'That's good, son. I just wanted to know ... and what are you doing tomorrow evening?'

'Tomorrow evening?' I asked king Solomon, rather embarrassed, and you know why. 'Tomorrow evening? ... Er ... I'm not doing anything special. ... I shall be at home. I shall go to bed, I've been feeling rather tired these last few days. I shall rest. Why do you want to know?'

And he went away.

I must explain: at that time, when a young man from our village had a fiancée, it was his duty to go from time to time to visit her, that is to say more especially her parents, since in theory he was not supposed to have so much as a peaceful chat with his fiancée. Usually some friends went with the young man, and in this way became known to the girl's family. So, on the day when the young man, for any reason, couldn't go himself, his friends had the right to take his place, to pay court to his girl. On the evening when I decided to go to Agatha's rather than to Tanga's, certain of my friends could therefore go in my place to my future in-laws, without it seeming odd to anybody. That is what happened.

King Solomon sent my friends to Tanga's, at the usual time for the evening visit. With what orders? You will learn that shortly. Ebanda, Toko, and of course my cousin Ekéké, were the 'official agents' of this nocturnal mission. But, for once, they were accompanied by four other young men from our village, who didn't themselves go to Tanga's, but awaited developments in the street.

Tanga's house wasn't right on the street. You left the street and took a path across a garden planted with 'Senegal cassava', which is what the Douala women call this kind of cassava; why I don't know. Finally, at the bottom of the garden, you came to Tanga's house; a raised floor of beaten earth, fragile walls of straw matting, a roof of corrugated iron, it presented the proud appearance of a man in easy circumstances. All around it, in a compound of sandy white soil, were the smaller dwellings of his wives. He had three. It was in this compound that in fine weather and on moonlit nights, we were in the habit of sitting with Fanny's parents and talking until a late hour. And on that evening, Ekéké and his companions behaved in the usual way. They had dinner with Tanga, and then came the long evening during which they told all kinds of stories. At the end, Tanga's wife yawned.

'You are sleepy, wife? What is this sleepiness just when it's time to shut up the hens, as if you had no strength?'

She tried to stay awake, to prove to her husband that she wasn't . . . a bird anxious to get to bed early. But finally, sleep won the day. Wonjè, Fanny's mother, nodded her head, involuntarily, like a person who is drowsing and can't help himself.

'Go to bed,' said her husband. 'Don't stay there making us sleepy too.'

'And we too,' said Toko, one of my friends, 'we too must be going; it's getting late . . . Fanny, won't you come with us as far as the garden gate? Just that far, to the street, and then you can come back.'

'Oh,' said Fanny, 'with all these ghost stories you've been telling, I'm frightened now, I'm frightened, and I don't know how I'm going to sleep tonight, and you ask me to see you on your way?'

'Come now, Fanny,' said father Tanga. 'You're growing up, you're engaged to be married, and you pretend to be afraid as if you were a child. You must learn good manners: when strangers come to see you, you must go back with them a little way, or they are entitled to think that you're badly brought up, and it's I, your father, who would be shamed in the end.'

At these words, Fanny got up promptly, while her father went into the house, with a recommendation to the girl to come back quickly so as to take in the benches and chairs in case it rained during the night.

The young men walked beside Fanny.

Soon they reached the street. And then everything changed. Toko and Ebanda seized the girl, one arm each, firmly, while my cousin Ekéké, whistling a tune agreed in advance, called the other fellows hidden in the bushes. They all suddenly surrounded Fanny, who was frightened. She tried to shout, to call for help, to cry, but in vain; somebody put a hand over her mouth, and nobody in the vicinity heard any kind of appeal for help.

'Hurry up, hurry up,' said one of the young men.

'We're taking you to our village tonight, Fanny,' announced Ekéké; 'from now on, you're the wife of the Law, you're our wife. Come on then, let's take her away.'

They had no difficulty in carrying little Fanny and in

getting her away from her village. As soon as they were out of reach of possible pursuers, they put her back on her feet:

'Now, you must run with us,' they ordered.

Run . . . and run she did: both arms firmly held by two men. Fanny did her best. And as she ran, she wept, and wept.

They arrived in our village about midnight. I was not yet back. As soon as they were inside the limits of our village, they began to shout: 'Ou-ou-ou-ou . . . Ou-ou-ou-ou . . . We have her, the bride, we have brought her back, the Law's wife . . . Ou-ou-ou-ou . . .' Immediately, from every house, people ran out to see the bride of the night. And all, more or less wide awake, set about welcoming Fanny, and offering her the customary advice: 'Bride, don't be selfish; bride, be kind, don't be selfish . . . Ou-ou-ou-ou . . .'

The noise of the crowd reached me just as I was returning from Agatha's village. As I drew near my house, I saw that it was already full of people . . . and when I say full, you can't imagine how full. And what a racket . . . so much shouting and singing and empty boxes beaten like drums, all of which completely covered Fanny's sobs. I managed to make a way through the crowd and to reach my house. I found Maa Médi sitting beside Fanny, who was in tears.

'My daughter,' said Maa Médi, seeing me, 'here is my son. He is your husband. Stay here with him, to serve him and give him children, many children.'

I paid no more attention to Fanny than when I used to go and see her parents, supposedly to pay court to my fiancée. For me she was a little girl, and the main thing was to finish her training until, later, she began to give me children. In any case, I thought, it was Maa Médi who had engineered this premature marriage; now it was her job to take Fanny in hand and make her into a real wife worthy of her son. So when everybody, worn out by some two hours of hellish din and bustle, finally decided to go to bed, Fanny went to spend the night, not in my room, but safe and sound with Maa Médi.

When Tanga didn't see his daughter come back as usual that night, he guessed that something had happened. Immediately he went to give the alarm to his brother Njiba, who was in charge of Fanny's marriage. There is nothing to be done in such a case, when it has been impossible to prevent the abduction of a girl by the people of her fiancé's village. If he had known, Tanga would have forbidden Fanny to see the visitors on their way; that would have been the only way to avoid what had just happened. He hadn't done so, trusting in the good manners of his guests. Now it was too late, there was nothing anybody could do.

'She is married, our daughter,' said Njiba, half-asleep; 'married, before those people have finished paying the money they owe us ... but she is married and there is nothing we can do ...'

Tanga and Njiba, each in his own place, spent as peaceful a night as if nothing serious had taken place. The next day they invited the women of the village to come to my house, to 'weep for their daughter'. They came in a crowd. I assuaged their grief with 'a little money to buy cooking salt and tobacco for the community'. Fanny, of course, stayed with us.

6

King Solomon set down the last stone at the foot of the orange tree and went to wash his hands in the dirty water contained in half of a badly sawn barrel. Maa Médi was returning from her plantation, accompanied by Fanny. They were both very tired: a full day's work, in the hot sun of this month of December, was not particularly amusing. Fanny was busy learning from my mother her future role as mistress of the house. I didn't see her often, for I continued to go deep-sea fishing, and to visit Agatha . . . when she was willing, for now that I was married in the sight of everybody, Agatha no longer made herself available to me as she had done before. That is another story, which we shall come back to later.

My mother saw an enormous heap of stones at the foot of the orange tree. She almost said nothing to king Solomon. She had a lot of respect for this man, who had helped her son avoid the shame of taking a partner of undesirable notoriety. So she almost didn't speak, believe me. But this heap of stones, there at the foot of the orange tree, meant that the tree would die very shortly. These cement blocks had already dried up two orange trees in the village, and Maa Médi was anxious that this tree, which I had planted myself, should not suffer the same fate. That is why she spoke:

'Solomon, you're at it again, putting your bricks at the foot of this orange tree. You know that cement is fatal for these trees, and you're doing it again here; don't you want us to have even one ripe orange during the hot season?'

'Woman,' replied the king, 'you're wrong on two counts: first, they are not "my bricks" as you are pleased to call them. For you know I'm as poor as you, and that in consequence I could never afford to buy cement to make blocks. You know that it's Big-Heart who gave me this work to do. You're wrong again when you accuse me of wanting to kill your orange tree. Heaven didn't give me hands to destroy, but to create. Don't you all call me, in the village, "the builder king" . You see then? I tell you this whole business concerns, solely, Big-Heart, who wants to finish building his stone house at all costs.'

Maa Médi admired the wisdom of the king's reply. But she told herself that that would not be the end of the matter: she would go herself to see uncle Big-Heart, as soon as he returned from his work.

'Yes, I'll go and see him this evening, in his stone house,' promised my mother, with an acid note in her voice.

Then she put down the bundle of firewood and went into her house to get the evening meal.

Fanny had been with us for some time. Various things had happened which I shall not relate here, for the simple reason that most of them have nothing to do with the small story of my private life. But let us return to the end of the day of king Solomon.

The king washed his hands. The cement disappeared, but the blackness of the skin on the back and the whiteness of the palms remained, in spite of the bit of Marseilles soap. Then the king wiped the sweat from his brow with a dirty handkerchief. The day was over. He took up his jacket, very threadbare, and smelling of humid sunlight. The king put in one arm and felt something cold inside. Frightened, he threw the jacket some distance with a quick movement, and automatically wiped the hand which he had tried to put into the sleeve. A frog found its way through the labyrinthine folds of the jacket, and jumped out. The king smiled and uttered a sigh of relief. It was not a snake, as he had at first thought, it was only a frog, a frog which couldn't bite . . . 'How afraid I was,' the king admitted to himself. 'This jacket will certainly be able to tell more than one tale.'

Solomon, the king-builder of houses, could also make up stories of all kinds, sometimes out of nothing, with an unequalled interpretation assumed . . . even when there had not been a frog in the sleeve of his khaki jacket. Already the little creature had disappeared into the damp grass of the compound, and already it had grown considerably larger in the lively memory of Solomon. He had never before seen such a big frog. And then, you should have seen how aggressive it was . . . perhaps it had not been an ordinary frog at all. You saw so many strange things in our little village . . . The king immediately invented a solid and impressive background for this ordinary affair of a frog which had sheltered from the sun in the sleeve of his jacket, when Dicky came by.

'Good evening, king. How are you?'

'Oh, leave me, Dicky, if you only knew what has just happened to me. Oh, leave me, leave me . . .'

'But you seem upset. What's the matter?'

'Dicky, belive me, my father certainly lived longer than I have, but I do assure you that I have seen far more than he. Yes, far more extraordinary things . . .'

'But at least tell me what's the matter.'

'Oh, it's something strange, Dicky. How can I tell you all that's just happened to me? Listen and answer me: have you ever seen a frog?'

'A frog?'

'Yes, a frog.'

'Oh, king Solomon, I can't read, I didn't go to school, I don't speak French, like Big-Heart or Ekéké, but all the same, allow me to tell you that I know what a frog is. What a question . . .'

'No, don't get annoyed, Dicky. I'm not asking you that to annoy you. I simply wanted to make sure that I wasn't dreaming just now. Tell me: what's a frog like?'

'What's it like . . . what's it like . . . but, nothing . . . except another frog.'

'Yes, that's true, that's true. Why am I so stupid? And do you think, Dicky, that it's cold, a frog?'

'Cold, like any other frog. I tell you they're all alike.'

'But tell me: have you ever seen a frog grow longer?'

'Grow longer?'

'And change its face?'

'Change its face? What are you saying, king Solomon?'

'And getting ready to say: "I am so-and-so's frog".'

'You're mad, king Solomon, you're mad. What are you saying?'

'Yes, exactly, that's what I've just seen. And you know, king Solomon wouldn't invent such a tale ... and I could even, if you like, tell you whose frog it was.'

Dicky felt almost dizzy. He could hardly understand what king Solomon was saying when he went on:

'You see my jacket, Dicky, I ask you if you can see my jacket?'

Dicky was more and more bewildered. Night was falling. The time for fantastic and magic occurrences was approaching, its approach hastened under this orange tree by the king's strange tale.

'You see my jacket? You see, it was out of this jacket that the frog I'm talking about came. Now, look around you ... there's nothing here which would lead you to think that a frog would come and live so far from the river. What's more, the grass is short, and if there had been a frog before the event I'm telling you about, I should certainly have seen it and I should have stopped it crawling into my jacket. Now, a few minutes ago I came to get my jacket, and I felt something cold inside. I threw the jacket on the ground, and what did I see coming out of one sleeve?'

'A frog?'

'Yes, a frog ... but a frog such as I should never wish you to meet in your life ... a fat, completely black frog, which turned towards me as it came out of my jacket, stopped, stared at me, and began to grow longer and longer, while its face changed. And in the end, it was so changed, that its face had all the features of a real human face ... a face that you and I know well. And it was then that the frog

78

opened its mouth to tell me who owned it; but I tell you that that was unnecessary, for you could guess immediately from its face: you've never seen such a likeness . . .'

'And what did it say?'

'Nothing.'

'And so who does it belong to?'

'Come on now, Dicky, I tell you it wasn't a frog of the kind one usually sees, and then I tell you it was like somebody we know well, you and I, and you still ask whose it was? Nobody here can afford a magic frog except our brother Big-Heart . . .'

'If you still call him your brother, that's your business. But personally, after all he's done to us. I no longer regard him as a brother. You can't behave like that just because you want to build a stone house. After all, what's so wonderful about a stone house?'

'And do you know, Dicky, he makes me work at building his house, just as a white would make me work: he's killing me with work for almost nothing. And every evening, as soon as he gets back from his office, he comes to check what I've done during the day . . . as if he didn't trust me. Really, having a stable job in the town has gone to his head. You can say that all that's his own affair; but look what he's done to us: that large piece of land which he sold and which didn't belong to him, you remember that?'

'And he spends all the money he got out of it on himself . . .'

'I tell you,' concluded Solomon, 'that he has a magic frog which is so like him that he'll be hard put to deny it. If you pass on the story of my strange adventure to anybody else, don't forget to add that the frog itself spoke, to state its allegiance to Big-Heart. These magic frogs they have all the faculties to make them supernatural animals.'

It is unnecessary to say that all this was part of a slanderous campaign started a few days earlier against my uncle Big-Heart. It couldn't be otherwise. My uncle, this man who could read and write, and who thought only of living in European style, had already once before provoked a certain amount of reaction among the inhabitants of our village. But never before had he managed to unite against him a coalition like today's. For this time his enemies came from outside the limits of our village; they were to be found in the neighbouring villages, and particularly in that of Agatha Moudio, where her father uttered endless curses against 'this European in our midst who had forgotten to turn white and who sold the land of his fathers without asking the opinion of his fellows'. That had, in fact, been the latest act on the para-European programme of uncle Big-Heart. On the boundary of Agatha's village and ours was a piece of land, which nobody, so far, had found it useful to claim. So one day, a Syrian trader, confident in the commercial possibilities of this land, came to see the inhabitants of the village, to ask them to sell it to him. And uncle Heart, whom we had nicknamed Big-Heart because he loved big things, without saying anything to anybody, had negotiated alone with the Syrian, and had sold him the land, without any further formality. Just the kind of thing to avoid if you don't want to unleash the anger of the villagers. It's not that we obstinately refuse to sell land – in any case I wonder what land would remain to our people if they succeeded in selling it all to strangers from Syria or elsewhere – but we like to see the whole village involved in the transactions . . . and above all, we don't like to see one person spending on himself all the money from the sale of a piece of land, be it large or small. And because uncle Big-Heart had failed in respect for his fellows, everybody held it against him that he got rich at the expense of the community and was spending the money on himself. After all, just because uncle Big-Heart could read and write and talk to foreigners, he had no right to neglect his brothers. He had not acted in a brotherly way, and they were preparing to make it clear to him, in one way or another, that in this village which he had consciously chosen to ignore as unimportant, he could no longer claim to have brothers. You heard just now, when my mother pointed out to king Solomon that 'his cement blocks would kill the orange tree', he had said, 'I tell you this whole business concerns only Big-Heart, who wants to finish building his stone house as soon as possible.' And Maa Médi had promised in an acid tone that she would go and see this uncle Big-Heart, who was not content merely to build stone houses with other people's money, but also wanted to kill a tree without which we shouldn't be able to quench our thirst in the hot weather.

As for the tale of Big-Heart's magic frog, it was immediately a howling success. Nobody among us was better qualified as a publicity agent than Dicky. And the emotional state he was worked up into by this terrible tale merely accelerated its spread; this was rapid, from mouth to mouth, and the next day all the villages in the district knew that uncle Big-Heart had a magic frog. The fact is that nobody knew what a magic frog was like, for the simple reason that only king Solomon had seen one; and you know as well as I do that the one he had seen coming out of his jacket was no different from the frogs which you and I know, whether or not they are magic. This didn't prevent everybody from being able to describe in detail this frog of uncle Big-Heart's, 'the most terrifying of all the frogs on earth'.

Some nine days after the strange adventure of which king Solomon had been the only witness, Dicky, he who had undertaken to spread the news, lay dying in his house without out anybody ever being able to tell what he died of. You sometimes meet men and women who tell you, with complete conviction, that there is no such thing as sorcery, that it is all 'tall stories', and other such blasphemies. We have not, in our tongue, the word which is used in other languages to explain the inexplicable juxtaposition of certain facts: coincidence doesn't exist for us, and nobody believes in it. It must in any case be admitted that, in a little village like ours, the death of Dicky, just after he had betrayed the secret of a sorcerer, was difficult to classify as coincidence. This mischance gave us all a lot to think about; but was it really necessary to think? No, each of us believed, almost automatically, that the man who had killed Dicky, the only person who had a definite motive for doing so, was uncle Big-Heart.

This time he had gone too far; the people's anger reached its peak and one morning they besieged my uncle in his house, to prevent him from going to work. There was a crowd of men from our own and the near-by villages.

'You won't go to work today, Heart. You owe us some explanations, and we shall pass judgement ourselves if need be.'

It was terrifying, such a visit in the morning . . . because Dicky was dead? And what if it was not uncle Big-Heart who had led his spirit away into the impenetrable world of witchcraft? What if he had died his death, simply because life had had enough of him, and he was being called to the life hereafter? Such are the questions you may ask me, and I shall have to answer that, with us, no death is ever natural. It's always the work of a sorcerer. And this time, no mistake was possible: it was uncle Big-Heart who had caused Dicky's death.

'I've done nothing, I've done nothing, I tell you again. I didn't kill him. He was so dear to me, hi, hi, hi,' (he wept) 'that I should never have dreamed of doing such a thing, even if I had the power . . .'

'Perhaps you want to make us believe that you don't have the power? And Mother Mondo, who finished *her* off, if it wasn't you?'

'No, no, I didn't do that. Mother Mondo, think of all she did for me . . . I could never have done that . . . hi, hi, hi, she died without even saying farewell, poor Mother Mondo. I didn't kill her, believe me . . .'

All that Mother Mondo had done for him . . . what an argument. You know that in this infernal realm of witchcraft the sorcerers destroy precisely those people who are dear to them. Such is their law. All that Mother Mondo had done for him . . .

'Really, you take us for idiots, Heart, yes, you think we are idiots.'

Then the men began filing past him, in the big room where they were gathered, and each pronounced his sentence:

'You have caused the disappearance of far too many people round here,' said Chief Mbaka. 'You deserve that the bell should toll for you, in your turn. Seize this man and take him outside . . .' he ordered the others.

Uncle Big-Heart protested; he tried to defend himself but he was led away just the same. The men asked the women and children to remove themselves, for the sight of what was about to happen was not for them. In any case, the women had no part in all that: their job was to go and weep for Dicky, whose body was still lying in his house.

The men went under a big tree, on the village green. There they made uncle Big-Heart sit on a flat stone. They placed on his head a plank of hard wood about a metre long. And then they began putting stones on the plank, big stones, heavier and heavier stones, while two men ensured the balance of the plank by holding it firmly on my uncle's head. And each time a new stone was added on the plank, Mpondo-the-two-ends came forward and asked uncle Big-Heart:

'Tell us, tell us quickly, unless you want to die: you were the assassin, weren't you?'

The man made no reply. And immediately a new stone was added, heavier than the one before. My uncle's neck must

have been of a special build, for it endured the torture for a
long time. But aunt Adela knew that he wouldn't be able
to stand it for ever. She refused to go and mourn Dicky as
Chief Mbaka had ordered. She ran off towards the town,
saying in a loud voice that she would never set foot in our
village again until the men who tortured her husband were
punished. And the ordeal continued. We thought that aunt
Adela had run away for good, and that we should never hear
of her again. Far from it: she reached the town, found her
husband's place of work, and there did her best to explain
to uncle Big-Heart's boss that he was being killed. Immediately this man, who was already worried that my uncle had
not arrived for work although it was ten o'clock in the
morning, telephoned the police commissioner, M. Dubous.
You will remember him, the one who had come to have me
arrested one day when I had demanded money for salt for
the community. As soon as he heard what was happening he
jumped into his 'black maria' and arrived in the village an
hour later, giving us no warning of his arrival. The show
under the tree was still going on. I can't understand why
uncle Big-Heart wasn't already dead; indeed at times his
incredible physical resistance makes me seriously think that
he must have some magic power, if not of the kind he was
accused of having, at least of a less offensive nature, more . . .
for self-protection.

In the twinkling of an eye policemen surrounded the
square, and immediately all the men present were handcuffed. They had begun, naturally, by releasing uncle Big-
Heart from his heavy burden of stones. The other men, their
wrists handcuffed, were invited to get into the police van.
Most of the elders of our village were involved, headed by
Chief Mbaka, since he had been directing operations. Yes,
they were all there, almost all. And if I tell you the name of a
single one of them who was not among the prisoners, you
will say I'm a liar. And yet it's true: the instigator of the

whole affair, the only man in the place who had ever had the opportunity of meeting the famous magic frog, whose imagination went so far as to make people believe that this frog looked like uncle Big-Heart, yes, I tell you, king Solomon was not taken with the others in this raid. For that day, his extraordinary wisdom had made him 'ill, very ill', and he had had to shut himself up in his house during the whole shameful spectacle which you have just been watching.

The others were tried. None of them could be persuaded that he had done wrong, for they could not conceive that one of their brothers should be allowed to exterminate the community with impunity. The European judge who interrogated them almost went mad on hearing this tale about a magic frog: '*They* don't have that kind of thing', king Solomon was to explain to me later.

The judge sentenced them to four years in prison and decided that they should go and serve their sentences in the north of the country, at Mokolo. So it was that they went, almost all of them, the elders from our village as well as men from near-by villages, amongst whom I must mention, in particular, the father of Agatha Moudio.

7

When fate wants to mock men, it doesn't spare them. If you had come to our village about a year after this terrible affair, you would have realized this. For you would then have noticed that the two most important men, that is, the two oldest, who were still with us, were king Solomon and uncle Big-Heart. When I think of it again today I split my sides laughing, for I can see the expressions of these two men when they happened to meet in the single street of our village. There was king Solomon who, with his barely credible tale of a magic frog, had almost sent uncle Big-Heart to his death, and then the latter who, full of bitterness after what they had done to him, had sworn never again to speak to anybody in the village. 'Besides, I am leaving here, I'm leaving this cursed place,' he said frequently. But he never left, 'for,' he reminded himself, 'I was born here, and after all I consider I have already done a lot for the development of this village'. You can't deny it, he really had acquired the European way of looking at many things in life. Just listen to that: not to leave a village on the pretext that one has already done a lot to develop it . . . and all because he had built – or rather, had had built – half of a stone house, which he was already living in while he waited for the other half to complete the whole. The other half? Building had stopped for a year, since 'the affair'. King Solomon had in fact decided to do no more work for uncle Big-Heart, whom he accused of owning a frog different from other frogs. Because, after all, the builder king remained convinced that an ordinary frog could not have been in his jacket sleeve that day, when there was not even a river near the place where Solomon was working. 'His house? Oh, well, he can build it himself,' he had said. And when he was asked: 'But king, if you don't work what will you live on?' he replied, quite naturally, 'In this village, all the children are my children, so *I* shan't die of hunger as long as they work.'

And now, king Solomon lived in peace, with no cares at all . . . and each of the children of the village (his children) from whom he asked food and drink, hastened to give him what he asked, the more so because he had gradually become 'the only elder we have left'.

Since Dicky's death, we were all convinced that uncle Big-Heart was a redoutable sorcerer, and we feared him accordingly. The truth is that a village such as ours always needs someone to be in awe of, a man wrapped from head to foot in the secrets of black magic. Now you know that Eya, the husband of Mother Evil-Eye, he whom everybody used to fear, was in prison. So somebody was needed to replace him, and uncle Big-Heart was cut out for that. Fortunately, he was content to say that he was leaving 'this cursed village', but he never did so. I say fortunately, because otherwise we should have been obliged to consider king Solomon as a sorcerer of the first rank. That, I confess, would have been hard for us all, for in reality, the king builder, teller of tragic tales, was hardly cut out to be a magician.

After some time our village began to get used to its new look. The women got tired of weeping for their husbands who were away for so long. Soon, those of them who were still far from old began to console themselves ardently with immoral young men, either from our village or from surrounding villages. Their scandalous conduct went as far as the conception of children, to all of whom was given, later, the name 'Eboa', which means prison. This name will always remind the fathers of the four years they spent in prison, during which they hardly expected to find that they had acquired children on their return to the village. Such is life. But you must believe me when I tell you that these very pregnancies (oh, there were only three all told) were another irony of fate. Just imagine that with their real husbands these three ladies had never been able to have a child. People had often accused Mother Evil-Eye, saying it was she who prevented the village women from conceiving. And now, in the absence of their husbands, and in spite of the continued presence of Mother Evil-Eye, these good women had begun to have children. It was fantastic.

Fanny was still at Maa Médi's learning her future role as a wife. She went to the fields with my mother, worked all day with her, gathered firewood, and came back in the evening, exhausted after a day in the burning sun. Maa Médi was also teaching her to cook, and telling her my favourite dishes: 'If you want to make your husband mad one day,' she would tell her, 'give him Senegal cassava to eat with salt, and tell him there's no more fish in the house . . .' A strange way of teaching, you may think, and yet, it's true, my mother was right. I couldn't bear not having any fish in the house, for the good reason that I knew all the tricks of the trade to avoid shortage. 'If we haven't any more meat, I forgive you, I'm not a hunter; but if we run out of fish . . .' Maa Médi also gave Fanny all sorts of hints to help her keep her husband: 'If you can't prepare milled rice properly, my girl, you will have to go back to your parents. My son can't stand badly cooked milled rice; but by staying with me you can be sure of giving *La Loi* satisfaction.' So Fanny was gradually discovering what a difficult husband I was where good food was concerned; and Maa Médi, who loved her very much, taught her how to deal with difficult husbands. Soon, as the training in domestic science was drawing to an end, Maa Médi went to tell king Solomon that she wanted 'to return his wife to her son'. The wise king then advised her to invite all the women in the village, 'those who have a good heart, and sincere good wishes to express. Above all, you mustn't forget to invite Eye,' insisted the builder king.

The ceremony was fixed for the following Sunday. 'Sunday just after the arrival of the white hunters. Then, while they're in the forest, the village will be peaceful, and everything will go off well.'

Maa Médi made exhaustive preparations. She got a friend to help her and one of my aunts, who came specially from my mother's village. That Sunday men and women gathered in my house. They had not invited uncle Big-Heart, or his wife, my aunt Adela, who had returned to the village a few months before, following her flight on the morning of the terrible affair. It was thought that neither she nor her husband had a kind heart, and that any wishes they might express would not be sincere. It was not the first time that Fanny had collected a crowd in my house – you remember the night she got herself kidnapped. Today there was just as much noise as on that night, but that didn't stop us suddenly hearing the first two Sunday morning shots. The white hunters were already collecting the monkeys from the trees. This time Ekéké was not with them: my cousin was in fact anxious to be present at Fanny's entry into my house. 'It was I who went to get her. So I must be there to see how she takes possession of her home,' he said. I thought he was right to abandon the white hunters in my favour. After all, perhaps they didn't need him that Sunday, to talk to the forest monkeys . . . In a corner of the room where we were, in my house, three large stones had been placed on the ground. They made up the hearth, in which firewood had been laid. The bundles of twigs went between the three stones and met in the middle of the triangle at the top. Fanny, for the first time in her life, would light a fire in a hearth that was her very own, and which would remain hers as long as she was my wife.

'Women, and you, my children,' said king Solomon then, taking off his famous threadbare khaki jacket, 'we have come here to leave a wife under this roof. My daughter, Fanny, this is your home. When you arrived here a few months ago, – no, not just a few months, it's more than a year ago today – you were still only a child. From today you have become a girl capable of running a house, you are a woman. From now on, you will be the wife of our son here. I tell you he's your husband, this man, you understand me? I don't want somebody to come one day and tell me that you have refused to be a wife to *La Loi*. I say again, you have only one husband here, it is he. Here is your house. You must live here, work here, have children here . . .'

'My daughter,' said Mother Evil-Eye, 'I am sometimes accused of putting the evil eye on the women of this village. But I beg you to believe that I have looked on *you* with a very favourable eye since you came to us. I wish that you may continue to please me. Besides, I am not the only one here who thinks that you are a wife made for this village, and not for any other, even if elsewhere people are richer than they are here. Riches are nothing, my daughter. What you need in life is a good heart. You have a good heart, and we are fond of you, and you will be very happy here. You will see. Don't listen to the evil tongues of this village. I do no harm to anybody. I don't have a chance, they are all afraid of me, as if I were a witch. I can't harm anybody. Live here; work for our son; give us food when we are hungry; and don't have anything to do with the stories you hear; if you go to the public-fountain, draw your water and come home and cook food for your husband. If you keep both ears open to the gossip in this village you won't . . .'

'Woman,' interrupted king Solomon, 'that's enough. Today is not the day for long speeches. Women talk too much. We don't want to stay here till tomorrow morning. Médi, give your son his wife, as is fitting. "Hand over" his wife into his hands.'

Then Maa Médi took Fanny's right hand in hers and they both approached me.

'He-he-he,' shouted my mother joyfully. 'Tell me again that I'm only a poor female, tell me again that I've done nothing on this earth, and that I have nothing in the world. Tell me again that I've no right to be alive . . . who will speak?'

'Nobody,' replied the women in chorus. 'Nobody will speak.'

'If anybody has anything to say, let him speak now. I

show you the object of my joy: see now a poor woman who brings into the world an only child, I say an only child, as I show you one finger of my hand. And one fine day, she finds she has two children, and both are hers . . . yes, her very own. Which of you has something to say?'

'Nobody,' the women repeated.

'I am not a poor woman, said Maa Médi. 'I am not a childless woman. It wasn't one child that I brought into the world. It's you who can't count. I tell you: I have two children . . . which of you has something to say?'

'Nobody,' replied the chorus of women.

'Yes, *I* have something to say,' said an unexpected voice. It was aunt Adela's.

She came in, followed by her 'evil sorcerer of a husband', uncle Big-Heart.

'I too have something to say,' stated my uncle. 'I want to say that all that you're doing here is unjust. The Law's marriage is the marriage of all of us. You have no right to celebrate it without inviting us. You, Solomon, I didn't intend to speak to you again, because of what you did to me. But it's no use, you remain my brother. And then, my conscience is clear. I have something to reproach myself with, but it's not for being a sorcerer with a talking frog. No, I am not a magician. What I reproach myself with is that I took advantage of the fact that I can read and write, to sell to a stranger a piece of land which didn't belong to me more than to the rest of you. You made me pay dearly. I think it's time to put a stop to this business. Let it not be the faithful companion of our life, as death is the eternal companion of man. I was born in this village. I shall stay here all my life, and I don't intend to be ignored at moments as important as this one, and I won't have people avoiding me on the pretext that I'm a sorcerer with a strange frog, which I've never seen with my own eyes. So, I have something to say before you give the Law his wife. Solomon, and you other men here present, and I'll say the same before everybody when our brothers return from the distant land where "they" have sent them, I ask your pardon for what I did . . . and to take me back among you . . .'

King Solomon was very afraid he would not know what to say after this unexpected speech. At last he found some words to mutter:

'It's true . . . it's true that this affair of the land was at the bottom of all the rest. You had treated us as if we were inferior, people of no importance, not to be let into any secret, and above all, as if we had no right to be interested in our own affairs . . . I held it against you, personally, my brother Heart . . . and the others also. But all that . . . is . . . is past, since you recognize, yourself, that you acted badly towards us. The Almighty will soon bring our brothers back here, and we shall go on living as if nothing serious had happened. Life is like that, full of pitfalls. One must walk upright, whatever the circumstances; otherwise, one stumbles and falls. We didn't walk upright, we stumbled and we fell. That is all, there is no other explanation for what happened. After all, if I'm still in this village, if I didn't go with the others, it was pure luck that brought it about . . . otherwise, I too would be at Mokolo. Stay with us, brother, stay among us, and let's forget it all . . .'

The women were already shedding floods of tears. They were weeping for the absent, they were still weeping for Dicky, poor Dicky, whose death started the terrible affair. 'But what sickness can he possibly have died of, when he was brimming over with health?' they were asking themselves. For in the present circumstances, they could no longer accuse my uncle Big-Heart of having caused his death, with the help of his strange frog.

Aunt Adela also was accepted back among the women, and they went on with the ceremony, which had been interrupted by the arrival of the couple.

'You see, my daughter,' said Maa Médi to Fanny, 'you see, that's how we live in this village. If one day you have a grievance against somebody, you're not entitled to hold it all your life. Everything must be sorted out and return to normal, otherwise, it's not life . . . Now, I will give you your husband. Come.'

She took Fanny's right hand in hers again and both came towards me.

'Get up, my son,' she said to me.

I got up. I was a giant beside Fanny.

'Open your right hand and show it to me,' ordered Maa Médi.

I obeyed the order.

'Oh, all you here present, shall I count?'

'Yes,' they all replied with one voice.

'Shall I count?'

'Yes.'

'Then,' said my mother, 'the Law, here is your wife. I give her to you, once, twice, three times, four times . . . nine times. Take her. And look at me, watch me carefully . . . I have nothing else to give you. Nothing, not in my hands, nor my eyes, nor at my feet, nor at my hips. Nothing . . . I have given everything.'

It was over. From now on, Fanny would live with me . . . my wife.

She began by lighting her fire, to reheat those of the dishes which were unappetizing when eaten cold. And we ate, and we drank, in the midst of endless speeches and laughter. And little Fanny was there, happy to become suddenly the mistress of a house that was all her own, in a village where, after all, life must be just as good as in her own village, down yonder, with her parents.

The day ended with the customary departure of the whites, who had returned from their monkey-hunt. Sundays in our village had not lost this picturesque side, in spite of

93

the events which had shaken us for months past. At all events, today Maa Médi would sleep peacefully. Her son was married, well and truly married. She need no longer fear the arrival of any loose-living girl, Agatha Moudio or anybody else. What she was forgetting, my dear good mother, was what she had told me once herself, when she was busy trying to persuade me not to marry 'this girl rejected by everybody'. What had she said? 'My son, when a woman wants a man, she's capable of doing anything to get him. And,' she had added, 'Agatha wants you . . .' The future, full of mystery, couldn't yet tell me whether Maa Médi was right or not. At the moment, I was married, finally, and the duties which awaited me now were of a quite different kind from those I had had to fulfil up till then.

'It's a different life, you know,' Maa Médi had warned me. Different . . . yes, how different . . .

Fanny's parents came to visit us from time to time, 'to see how we were getting on'. Their visits were expensive, for they were anxious that I should not imagine that I had taken Fanny like any girl I might have picked up in the street. No Fanny had left her parents' house to come to mine, and I had to say 'thank you' several hundred times to all the members of their huge family. And every time they came, I showed my gratitude by loading them with gifts. In principle, I need not have laid on my thanks quite so heavily, for you no doubt remember the words used by Njiba the day we went to ask the people of Deido to let me marry Fanny: 'We give you our daughter free of charge,' he had said. But of course, since the day when this apparent generosity showed its true face, I was condemned to make presents to any person claiming to be of Tanga's family, who might come to visit me. That will certainly go on all my life, but we won't talk about it. For this burden of compulsory generosity has its origins in a past which need in no way compel our attention at the present time. That is what king Solomon thinks too whenever he wishes to remind me that I must remain a man: 'You know, son,' he tells me, 'you must never cast your eyes back: heaven placed them on the front of the face so that they look at what is ahead. The time to come is not behind, it is ahead. If you would be a man, that is where you must turn your eyes.'

I promised to obey the wise advice of king Solomon, and I resolutely turned my eyes towards the mysterious future, which mocks the crazy plans of men. Even the men of my village . . .

'Fanny . . . Fanny . . . Fanny, but where is she then?'

'Here I am, Mother Eye. I answered as soon as you called, but you didn't hear me. Here I am.'

'Ah, there you are. Stay there, don't move from where you are. Last night, my daughter, I dreamed of you.'

Mother Evil-Eye had risen early, to come and tell Fanny she had dreamed of her. She hadn't gone to the public fountain before seeing Fanny. When one has dreamed of somebody, one doesn't go to the public fountain before having told them what one has seen in the dream and doing what is necessary to avert ill-fortune. Mother Evil-Eye picked up a big, smooth round pebble and threw it in Fanny's direction. That was all. The spirits seen in the dream could do nothing more against my wife at present.

'It doesn't do to neglect these things,' said Mother Evil-Eye. 'You modern children are beginning not to pay attention to these traditions, but believe me, they wouldn't have come down to us if our ancestors had not tested them over a long period. Come and see me at my house; I have something to tell you.'

When Mother Evil-Eye comes to see you early in the morning and says she has dreamed of you, and asks you to go and see her, you mustn't lose any time in going. For if she wants to have a private talk with you, at a time when she should be at the public fountain, collecting and passing on gossip, you must know that she likes you and that being the case, she only wishes you well. It's true; since the day when Maa Médi had handed my wife over to me, trained as she should be, it was obvious that Mother Evil-Eye had given Fanny her friendship. 'So much the better,' my mother had said; 'In that way, you're in no danger of getting a barren wife.' For you know that, in spite of her long defence that day, everybody in the village remained convinced that it was this old woman who controlled the births in our village. 'But then why,' I had asked Maa Médi, 'did she let three women conceive when their husbands were away?' And my mother answered, shrugging her shoulders: 'Why . . . why, don't you know that she's not averse to causing a bit of scandal from time to time?' A bit of scandal, my mother said. I'm still wondering today what is the dividing line between a big scandal and a little one. But, as Maa Médi said, better a woman who produces natural children than one who has no children at all. Perhaps one day we shall see just where this classification of women in order of preference can lead a man. For the moment, let us return to the morning of Mother Evil-Eye's dream.

She had seen Fanny during her sleep. Fanny was in great danger. A man, with a stomach such as only a dream can produce, had a grudge against her, and on the road to market,

96

barred her way with his enormous torso, preventing her from going on. Nobody knew where this far from ordinary man had come from. He wasn't like anybody in our village. (He certainly couldn't be like uncle Big-Heart, because since the other day he was no longer held to be a sorcerer.) It must be someone from another village, perhaps someone from Fanny's village? That was very possible, considering the ill feelings of 'those people' towards us, on account of the way we had brought Fanny to our village, without telling them.

'This fat man, my daughter, will not harm you . . . not at all, I can assure you. Stay calm; I am here, and I am at least as strong as that devil . . .'

Our people are accustomed to say that lies have short legs. Mother Evil-Eye had just proved this without meaning to do so. Do you remember what she had said the other day at my place: 'I am not a witch, although people are afraid of me . . .' and today, she was admitting to Fanny that she was as as strong as this 'devil' with the paunch, seen in a dream, who could be nothing but an evil sorcerer. Fanny was afraid when she heard Mother Evil-Eye talk like this. The woman guessed that the girl was afraid.

'No,' she told her, 'I won't harm you, my daughter. I have sworn to protect you, don't be afraid, nothing will happen to you.'

They went together into her house. A strange house, with a tiny front door and no windows at all. It was dark inside.

'Come in, daughter,' said Mother Evil-Eye. 'This house is yours . . . When my husband comes home, he will say the same.'

Fanny overcame her childish fear and went in. After all, why be so afraid? Witches are not evil when they present themselves as friends. Afraid? Of what? She went in, not without spitting lightly three times on the threshold of beaten earth. 'House, house, I am entering under your roof, don't harm my head,' she said very softly.

'Sit down, daughter, and listen to me carefully. I have a certain number of things to tell you that you must know. Everything is ready, sit down.'

Fanny sat down on a bench in the darkness, which was even deeper when Mother Evil-Eye had closed the only door.

'Take this herb ... blow on it three times ... that's good; now put it in your mouth and chew it. Chew it well, as if you were eating an excellent piece of meat. Chew well ... yes, like that. Now, swallow, swallow it all. That's good. Now take a mouthful of this water; wash your mouth out, and spit out the water on the floor.'

Fanny did as she was told. She couldn't do otherwise; she didn't see how she could do otherwise.

'With what you have just eaten, daughter, the fat man can do what he will, but he won't get you. You are now protected against any evil spell. But it's not finished, for we must now prepare your future.'

'What?'

'Yes, you know ... little things one must think of when one is newly married and has a husband whom other women's eyes can see. You can't hope to keep your husband for yourself alone if you don't take certain precautions. And of all the precautions, the most elementary is to open your eye. When I say "open your eye" I really mean open both eyes. And to see clearly, your well-opened eyes must be able to see. There are people with their eyes wide open who still scarcely see what is going on around them. I must open your eyes, daughter. And you know, if I do you this service, it means that I feel sympathy for you. You have never seen such sympathy, I can tell you. Stay there, don't move ...'

Mother Evil-Eye took two steps in the unbroken darkness, then came back to Fanny, carrying a long flat stone, which she placed in front of my wife. She looked and found another stone too, smaller and oval. 'These two stones, "the mother and the daughter" as we call them, are used to crush groundnuts or peppers. You put the seeds to be crushed on the long flat stone, "the mother", and you move "the daughter" over them, pressing hard, until they are quite crushed and the seeds reduced to powder or paste.' Mother Evil-Eye put a piece of bark on the 'mother stone'.

'This bark, daughter, I can't tell you from what tree it came. That is a secret. Crush it, crush it quickly, so that I can open your eyes with it. . .'

Fanny began to crush the bark, while the old woman was making a funnel with a banana leaf softened in a flame. When Fanny had finished the witch took the resulting paste, and put it in the funnel. She closed this by turning the rest of the banana leaf down over the paste. What skill . . . in the dark, Fanny thought. Then Mother Evil-Eye heated the lot in the still-warm ashes of the dead fire, and approached Fanny:

'Open your left eye,' she ordered; 'the left eye, I say, open it wide.' And she put three drops into the open eye.

'Oh, it stings, it stings, it will pierce my eye,' cried Fanny.

'But no, daughter, on the contrary, it will open your eye . . . why are you shouting like that? My goodness, didn't your parents think of doing this kind of thing before sending you to be married? Don't behave like a little girl here. Open the other eye now; quickly, so that the pain stops in both eyes at once.'

Fanny did as she was told, and shouted even louder when the drops fell. But it was nothing; now, she had both eyes open wide, open, and she could in future be at peace, sure that she would see if ever another woman tried to take her husband from her. In any case, if she ever met with such a misfortune, 'you have only to come and see me', said Mother Evil-Eye, 'and I will deal with the matter myself'.

Then the old witch took a calabash, took out the stopper,

and tipped it out in the palm of her left hand. A handful of toasted groundnuts came out.

'Eat some,' she said to Fanny, 'and you will see that they are not like the roasted groundnuts you used to be given at home. I prepared them specially for you this morning, following a recipe that I'll give you one day, when you're older. You will take this calabash, and every time you have a bad dream, eat a handful of the ground nuts when you wake. Only, you must understand: nobody else must be allowed to touch this calabash. Do you understand?'

Fanny promised that nobody but herself would touch the calabash. But that wasn't all. Mother Evil-Eye took out a bench and ordered Fanny to sit on it. Then she brought a rusty old razor blade, which had probably once been used by her husband, old Eya. The blade wasn't very sharp.

'Now I must purify your blood, for I want your path through life to remain clean, so that you walk without any fear.

She ordered Fanny to undresss, which she did, although the sight of the razor did little to reassure her. Then around the left ribs she made three cuts which hurt Fanny, who began to cry quietly, blotting out the witch's explanations.

'We're living in an age where evil spells are legion. Thanks to this first cut, they won't affect your blood. The second, daughter, will make you love everybody, and your enemies themselves will be dazzled and will no longer think of harming you. As for the third, it will cause you to have many children, and it will strengthen your blood, each time you are expecting a child. However, listen to me, listen carefully to the advice I'm going to give you: if you see on your path traces of urine, don't walk over them, or you will inherit all the sicknesses of the person who spread the urine. What's more, all that I have done to you or given you this morning would lose all its power. If you see a pregnant woman, don't look at her unkindly; but if you become pregnant one day, tell nobody but Maa Médi, your new mother, and me too. *I* have to know, to protect you, but I repeat, tell nobody else, you hear me? The days are past when women told all their friends they were expecting a child. The present times are bad and you must be careful. When you tell somebody you have a child in your womb, you can be sure you're risking miscarriage. Tell nobody. I haven't finished; when you go to work in the fields, if you hear an unknown voice calling your name, don't turn round, and above all, don't answer. There are evil spirits who go walking in the woods collecting people, and they later sell them at the slave market of Koupé. Be very careful about that. And finally, if you know one day that you are expecting a child, and if an elder from any village at all comes to ask you for cooking salt or pepper, answer him that men don't cook, and therefore he has no need of salt or pepper, and don't give him any. He is somebody trying to make away with the fruit you are carrying in your belly. Don't give him salt or pepper. Now, daughter, get dressed again and go away. Don't forget anything I've told you. I have finished for now but you must come back and see me this evening, a little after sunset . . .'

When Fanny got outside again with her calabash, the cuts still hurting her, she had the impression she had been living in another world.

'What magic, what magic,' she thought.

And yet she knew that all that Mother Evil-Eye had just done was necessary. She couldn't live in this village, and have children with her husband, in peace, unless somebody with the strength of Mother Evil-Eye helped her to overcome the difficulties of life. The forces that surround us here below are great. When one has the good fortune to have a friend with 'four eyes', one must consider oneself lucky. Mother Evil-Eye had 'four eyes', two that were for all to see, and two which she used to see things in the invisible world of black magic. She and her husband Eya were well known. It was said that in spite of their apparent poverty in our village, they were incredibly rich once night fell, when they were back among their colleagues the sorcerers. In this strange world of black magic, the blacks are far superior to the whites. They possess all that the whites possess in ordinary life, and much more: boats, trains, aeroplanes, two-storied houses, and goodness knows what else. The only law of their fraternity is that they must not reveal their knowledge, and they mustn't use it to the advantage of people who are not of the fraternity. Everything must remain secret, otherwise it's no longer magic – that's easy to understand.

On returning to Mother Evil-Eye's in the evening, 'a little after sunset', Fanny found a meal waiting for her. 'Eat first,' said the old woman, 'we'll do the rest later.' One can't refuse an invitation to eat. So Fanny sat down and ate with a good appetite, although she had already eaten at home. Afterwards, they went on to 'the rest'. Mother Evil-Eye undressed her:

'I want to wash you, so that you make a clean start in life.'

She took her behind the house; a large bowl was waiting there, white in the dark night, and full of water. 'And that isn't water from the public fountain, my girl,' remarked Mother Evil-Eye. 'Stand there; yes, there; don't move.' Then she got from somewhere some dried bark, which she threw into the bowl of water. A few seconds later she took some of this water in her mouth, filling out her cheeks, and she blew three times in Fanny's direction, like a mother elephant giving a shower to her baby. After that, she invoked several kinds of gods, and began again showering water out of her mouth on to Fanny. Finally, she told her she had finished and Fanny could wash herself now. She washed herself all over, from head to foot, so as to make a clean start in life.

Then the days began to go by, each less eventful than the other. Days, weeks, months, and still nothing new.

'It's odd,' my mother and Mother Evil-Eye said to each other. 'It's odd that she still hasn't spoken of her child . . . What's she waiting for then?'

What was she waiting for? I have no idea, but I can assure you that it certainly wasn't a child. For you know that I had not yet made up my mind to have a child with this girl of barely sixteen. She might be my wife but I didn't know her any the better for that. 'I must wait until she's older,' I told myself each time I felt a serious desire to commit an offence against a minor. And I went out 'for a walk'. That was the official excuse, for I know that you can easily guess where I went. Yes, I had Agatha Moudio under my skin, with all respect to Maa Médi. I confess that I no longer knew exactly where I stood with her, for since I had been 'really' married, she had decided that she would not always be available to me as she had been before my marriage, when she had 'been foolish enough to hope' that I was going to 'make my life' with her. No, she had changed now, and I thought it all the more a pity because my feelings for her had remained the same. At a certain point she had even gone back to her old tricks, with long outings of several days to the town, where she supposedly went to see her aunt, although I was convinced that that was not the truth. I really no longer knew where I stood with her. The truth was that, since my return from the fishing, my one idea was to go and see her again. And I was sad each time I got to her house and she wasn't there. There is no need to say that in our village, where nothing remained a secret, people knew that I was continuing to see Agatha Moudio. Not everybody, at least I suppose not, for my mother never came to reproach me about my behaviour, which she would certainly have done if she had heard anything at all. Oh, it's certain that she would have spent at least one morning raising her arms to heaven and praying that fresh rays of light would fall on my path. Thank goodness, Maa Médi didn't know that I was still seeing Agatha.

But among the people who did know was Toko, one of my friends who, on that memorable night, had kidnapped Fanny. Toko called himself my friend; and I considered him as such. That doesn't alter the fact that it was he who took it upon himself to be responsible for my wife's first child. Friends and wives are like that. When I would have sworn by all the gods in creation that Fanny hadn't yet been with a man, for the very good reason that I had left her in complete peace since we were married, there she was growing fatter in the middle, without telling me . . . slowly, but surely. Obviously, she said nothing to anybody, and it's easy to understand why: she couldn't say anything to Maa Médi or to Mother Evil-Eye, in case I came to hear of it. For if I had come to hear of it, I should certainly have had something to say; and I should have had good reason to have things to say about it, don't you think? So she kept quiet, and Toko continued to go to her every time that I myself was with Agatha. Life produces such situations . . . I told you that Fanny kept quiet. But our people are accustomed to say that a pregnancy is like a yam cutting: planted in the ground, at first, there is nothing to see; but as time passes, the tuber swells rapidly, and soon, it has the greatest difficulty in staying hidden underground. But when it's a question of pregnancy the women of our village don't wait to see a fat stomach to be convinced. So they started to show their surprise when Fanny got paler and paler. When a black woman turns pale, that means something. And then, dash it all . . . whoever heard of a pregnancy remaining a secret? Soon, Fanny's secret was out. *I* was the first to be surprised, when people came to wish me a son. What a business . . . Mother Evil-Eye asked Maa Médi if Fanny had told her about her pregnancy:

'And when did she mention it to me?' asked my mother by way of reply, adding: 'It's just what I told you the other day, these modern girls don't do things as we did in our day. Your daughter-in-law is expecting a child and she tells you nothing about it . . . nothing at all . . . and her husband, too, tells you nothing about what is happening . . . your own son conceals from you the joy which awaits you, and other people have to come from outside to tell you that you must prepare to be a grandmother one of these days . . .'

In spite of everything, my mother didn't turn Fanny out. On the contrary, she even showed her all that she had to do so that everything would go off well. She didn't yet know the truth about this pregnancy . . . the truth which I had only just learnt myself. It was the sudden disappearance of Fanny which led me to confess everything to Maa Médi. When she heard the news, she collapsed; she became quite ill.

'If I had known that it would come to this, I would never have bothered myself about your marriage . . . Lord, why did you put this girl Agatha in my son's way? I would not have forced him to an immediate marriage with this flighty little hypocrite Fanny.'

Maa Médi wept and wept, and once again I had to comfort her. But it remained to find Fanny. A wife who runs away has to be found, for she belongs to the village. Fanny had no right to leave our village, for any reason. Those of my friends who were still my friends helped me to find my wife. They also helped me to put Toko where he belonged: that was, beyond the pale, for nobody was willing to take on my wife's lover in his fishing crew. Toko had to leave the village, without exactly being asked to do so. He left, and never came back again.

Fanny had a difficult time in our village. Believe me, that wasn't my fault. I even did all I could to help her bear the burden of her child. But in a village like ours you couldn't get away with what she had done with impunity. There were songs about her, and also about her child, each of them loaded with malice which I found it difficult to bear myself. So, for example, they foretold the birth of a child 'without a head, or a neck, or a chin', all of which, be it said in passing, showed the stupidity of the authors.

Then came the happy event. And do you know, those people of Deido, Fanny's relations, once again had the cheek to come in a crowd 'to greet the baby and to show our village that it had chosen a good wife for me, for we had taken a wife who could produce children'. Can you believe that they were bursting with joy at the birth of the child, and that they made me pay them a goat and some red wine to toast the birth?

'And what is it?' I asked aunt Adela when she came out of the room where the delivery had taken place.

'It's a girl, and she bears my name,' replied aunt Adela.

'A girl . . . And they want a goat? What would they have wanted if Fanny had had a boy then?'

'Oh well,' said my mother who had just joined me, 'they would no doubt have asked for an ox . . . oh, never mind, son. The main thing is that your wife has given you a child. As for the goat and the rest, we'll see later on, and I expect we can arrange that.'

As you see, everybody, led by my mother, considered the child which had just been born as my child. Nobody was interested in knowing who the real father was: everybody knew that Fanny was my wife: she could only bring my children into the world, and not somebody else's.

'And then, my son, a child is a child,' king Solomon told me. 'A child is above all what it will be tomorrow. I tell you again, your eyes need not look backwards because they are in front. Behind you is the adultery of your wife, which you need not see. Before, there is what your daughter will become. That's what you must look at . . .'

I told myself that if ever the future could boast of being

full of anything, it could only be full of mysteries of all kinds. How many of these had it in store for me? I didn't know. But I resolved to obey the advice of the builder king: I turned my eyes to the future, with the childish hope of seeing what was borne on the moving waters of the deep.

9

It is not true that I had confessed everything to Maa Médi when I went to tell her that Fanny's child was not mine. Confess everything to my mother? I couldn't think of it, for it would have involved at the same time revealing my own unfaithfulness to Fanny. And if I was unfaithful to Fanny, then who with? With Agatha? My mother was hardly the person to tell that to. The poor woman would have been terribly upset; so I had chosen to be silent. Fanny's child was now born, and the celebrations for its birth were over. Life returned to normal.

The rainy season had started, with downpours and storms such as are known in only a few parts of the world. It was impossible to go fishing in such weather. People were living now on the tiny savings they had been able to make in the good season, and on the crops brought back to the village by their wives. And our village street too became a vital factor in our economy. It brought in money during the rainy season, this single street which went right through our settlement. Far-sighted young men helped it to become a really useful street. They had noticed that the mud produced by the rain could prevent the normal passage of cars. Such motorists as ventured during the bad season into this outlying suburb of Douala always managed, at some point, to get stuck in the mud. Then they asked the inhabitants for help. Our people are quite helpful; but they're not very keen on dragging their little bare feet through the mud, in the rain. So they made sure the imprudent drivers really had to beg for help, and only agreed to help them in return for payment. And they charged dearly for their services. This is how they discovered that this street 'which had come all by itself and installed itself in the village', could be used to feed the inhabitants at the height of the rainy season, when honest men were prevented from engaging in more honest ways of earning their living. So these far-sighted men made it their business to maintain the mud in the bad season. At night, they dug real ditches in the street and then skilfully re-covered them with earth, and by morning the street had assumed the peaceful appearance and the attractive look of a clean, well-kept roadway. In these conditions, the cars which arrived automatically stuck in the mud, and the driver must needs pay, and pay dear, to get out again. He paid for the outward trip, and then again on his return to the town. In this way, we no longer viewed the approach of the bad weather with the same horror as in the past, when we used to wonder if our stocks of provisions would last through the period of unemployment. And we blessed the street for coming and installing itself in the village, unasked by us. For I need not remind you that it was not we who had constructed this street, but the Administration, with a capital A. Today, when I hear people round me say that the street is a sign of progress, I wonder if they realize the truth of what they are saying.

But Dooh earned a prison sentence from his over-enthusiastic activity in this village street, after first getting a lot of money out of it. It happened in the most unexpected way. A fine blue car got stuck one morning. Immediately the crowd gathered, and volunteers came to ask what they would be paid for the effort needed to get it out. Dooh was the leader of the group of volunteers. Inside the car there was a black driver. They bargained, and then the men of goodwill set to work. The fine blue car came out of the mud with difficulty, was once again on firm ground, and went on its way ... as far as the next village, where its engine was heard to stop.

'That's odd,' said someone in the crowd, 'wasn't that the car belonging to one of the Sunday hunters?'

'But yes, yes, it's the car of the white with the mouthful of gold,' replied someone else.

'That's right, *he* was driving it the other day. That must be his driver ... but what can he have gone to Bonakamé for? He isn't a local, after all.'

Half an hour later the car came back through our village, and inevitably was once again stuck in the mud. That was when people, crowding round it, noticed inside ... Agatha. herself ... in one of the prettiest dresses I'd ever seen her wearing. She was sitting on the back seat. She was beautiful, beautiful as a sunny day. But what on earth was she doing there?

'So, Agatha,' said Dooh. 'So it's you, our sister, going off like this in a white man's car? Do you know the owner of this car, then?'

And the mocking crowd began to laugh until they were too much for Agatha and she, pushed too far, finally replied.

'What business is it of yours whether I know the owner of the car or not? You're always meddling in things that don't concern you. Do you want to know where I'm going? Well, don't torment yourselves, I'll tell you: I'm going to see the owner of this car. Are you satisfied now?'

No, I for one was not satisfied. I had seen Agatha the previous evening, and she hadn't told me that she would be going to the town the next morning, and now here she was, in a fine blue car, and she had the nerve to tell everybody, of her own accord, that she was going to see the owner of the car . . .

'Agatha,' I shouted, 'you shan't go there . . . I forbid you to go.' She looked at me and was about to say something, but Maa Médi immediately intervened:

'Son, my child, what has it to do with you? Just let this bad girl go off, in her car. Let her go where she likes, what difference does it make to you? She's not your wife and you needn't sully your lips by speaking to her . . .'

'That's enough, mother,' I said in a tone of rising anger. 'I tell you that's enough. In this village, you all insult this girl; she's not . . .'

'Let them say what they like, let them talk, *La Loi*. Don't bother about me; you heard what your mother said? I'm a bad girl. Go away, don't get involved in my life.'

'Dooh, Dooh, stop pushing this car, or I'll break it in pieces.'

I had shouted rather than spoken. Dooh knew what that meant, he knew I was angry, and that it would be unwise to cross me. Maa Médi tried again to stop me, but it was useless. Then she went away weeping, saying that Heaven had unfairly punished her by giving her a horrible son like me, who didn't even spare her the shame of being disobeyed in public. Dooh and his men were obliged to stop pushing the car.

'Dooh,' said Agatha then, 'if you don't push this car out right away, I shall tell the police that it's you who dig holes in the street to prevent cars passing unless people pay you. I repeat that I shall report it to the police if you aren't careful; d'you hear me?'

The crowd murmured. They hated Agatha, with all her faults, to which she now added the meanness of an informer. But the threat was too much, especially as Dooh and his men had already received the money asked for their services. Dooh gave me a look which signified: 'Brother the Law, it's not that I want to disobey you, but you hear what the girl says, you see the position I'm in; I wouldn't like to be caught so stupidly . . .' and they began pushing again. Then as I was about to grab hold of a rear door to get Agatha out of the cursed car, a hand rapped me on the shoulder. I turned round and saw king Solomon:

'Calm yourself, son, or I shall make an example of you in front of everybody,' he told me sternly.

Physically, I was stronger than king Solomon; but from the height of his position as a village elder, he governed my acts, and nobody would have forgiven me for disobeying him for a single moment. I immediately reverted to being like a little boy, just as at the time when the king himself, or others of our elders, took me on their knees to talk about the future. I said nothing, and there was nothing I could say. I went and shut myself up in my house, while the fine blue car took Agatha off to the town. I thought I should die of chagrin. My wife, little Fanny, tried to comfort me as best she could. Finally, she dared to look me in the eye, and say:

'If you love her, why don't you marry her?'

'It's not that I haven't thought of it,' I replied equally simply, 'but it's my mother who can't stand her. If you could persuade Maa Médi . . .'

From that moment, I knew that I could count on Fanny's intercession with my mother, and I again began to hope that I should perhaps one day become the husband of Agatha Moudio. 'Too bad if she's no good morally,' I told myself. 'In fact people who are any good are somewhat rare.'

The next day the police came to arrest Dooh. No, it wasn't Agatha who reported his activities to the police, contrary to what some of our people believed. It was the driver of the fine blue car who went and told his troubles to his boss, and that led to Dooh's arrest. In addition, this second scandal led to our village being put on the index by the colonial administrator responsible for us. 'The goings-on in that village are nothing if not extraordinary,' he was to write in his report at the end of his tour in occupied territory. And finally, our village obtained one of the first tar–sealed roads in Douala. At this stage of progress, we were entering on the active phase of life, the phase when only really honest work provides a living for honest men.

I hadn't confessed everything to Maa Médi when I had told her that Fanny's child, which was to be born a few months later, was not fathered by me. But now that the little girl had been born, and so much else had happened since, I thought I could afford to tell Maa Médi the whole truth. The incident in the street that morning, together with my wife's kindness, encouraged me to go and face my mother:

'You know,' I said to her one evening when we were having dinner together at her house, 'you know, you must forgive me for being sharp the other day. You are the only person in the world who can really forgive me. I'm very sorry about that incident, but *you* must understand that I'm grown up now . . .'

'You're grown up, you're grown up,' she interrupted, 'you're grown up when I still see you as quite small, quite small, as if I had just brought you into the world? You're grown up and you don't even know how to live with your wife, a wife ready to give you children . . .'

'So very ready to give me them,' I replied, 'that she even does so without my knowledge you must admit that's a bit much . . .'

That evening's discussion came to nothing. We had taken up our stands, and neither my mother nor I had any intention of giving way over our respective points of view. It was the first time that we hadn't ended an argument by reaching an agreement. 'Definitely,' thought Maa Médi, 'he has changed . . . the little child I knew has changed.' This idea was painful to her. It was painful to me not to admit that she was right, but I really felt that I was right. Why was she determined to treat me as the small boy she once knew? There must be an end to it, and I considered that I had been obedient long enough, and that the time had come for me to make my own decisions. And yet, the first decision that I wanted to make was to marry Agatha, and I didn't feel strong enough to do that without my mother's approval. What was I to do? I decided to go and see king Solomon and inform him of my intentions.

'Son, you will kill your mother if you do that,' he told me as soon as I had spoken of the main part of my plan.

'I'm only risking falling out with her,' I said, 'but she won't die of it: for you know she is very fond of Fanny. Now Fanny has promised to intercede with her.'

'I insist, son, I belive you will hurt your mother very much if you marry that girl. And then, who in the village would forgive you for taking a girl like that, one who has done so much harm to our community by causing Dooh to be put in prison . . .'

'It wasn't she who had him put in prison. She is certainly capable of many unmentionable things, but she wouldn't go and report that Dooh had made holes in the road to prevent cars getting through. I tell you she's incapable of that . . .'

'Oh, but you talk as if you knew her well, son? You haven't told me all I ought to know before going to see your mother, I can see. Come on now, speak, tell me everything.'

Tell him everything? It was difficult to say the least, but I did so, for I wanted him to be able to talk to Maa Médi in full possession of all the facts. When I had finished, the builder king gave me a friendly tap on the shoulder and winked. He had understood everything. The next day, he went to see Maa Médi, but it was in vain that he tried to make her understand how difficult it is to withstand love.

'For he perhaps imagines that she loves him . . .' said my mother. 'That's rich: she loves him, she loves him so much that she goes off to the town every day, and one can imagine what she does there . . . she loves him so much that she takes fine cars specially sent by white men, and it's not difficult to conceive what for . . . that's really rich: she loves him. Listen, king, you shouldn't approve this kind of thing, you know.'

'Woman, I agree with you that the conduct of this girl leaves much to be desired by a long way. But perhaps if she were in the hands of somebody who loved her, she would quickly change, she would become a different woman; perhaps she would even become a model of virtue?'

'And she would walk bent double under the weight of the keys of heaven,' went on Maa Médi. 'It's true, it has been known in the past, that's true; but today, it no longer happens anywhere, and especially not in this village. And then, king, tell me, who do you expect to bear the shame of having a daughter-in-law who has tasted life while she was still under age, in front of everybody, and who descends on my son when nobody else wants her? Who? Me?'

'I know, I know that you're afraid of what people will say. But you must understand what is going on in the Law's mind: he is telling himself that for his age, he has already shown himself very obedient. Admit that it's true: didn't he marry a wife we chose for him, without protest?'

'It wasn't we who chose her. It was his father who decided, and I think he had the right to decide his son's future. A good son can't refuse to let his parents think of his happiness.'

'Agreed, and he didn't refuse. He took this girl, although he would certainly have preferred not to have her as a wife. So he obeyed, like a good son. On the other hand, he points out that everything he has asked for has been refused him so far, as if he too hadn't the right to ask for anything. It isn't fair, Maa Médi; we can't go on regarding your son as a child for ever. He's reached the age where a man likes to stand up for himself in one way or another . . . tell me, is there any reason why he shouldn't have two or more wives? He is strong and brave, and he would be able to cope with them, don't you think?'

'Two wives? . . . I'm quite willing, though I'm not sure that the Law needs to marry two wives. But what I won't have, is that my son's second wife should be a high-class tart. He can marry any other woman in the world, but I repeat that I will not have Agatha Moudio . . . In any case, I still wonder what use a second wife would be here: a man takes a second wife when he is sure that he can't have a child by his first, or when he sees that she can't give him a son. We have to wait to see that. My son has only just married, and Fanny has already given him a daughter. She's not barren. Besides, you need only look at her mother, Tanga's wife: she has seven children, boys and girls . . .'

'Woman, all your arguments are good. I wouldn't dream of contradicting you. But you must understand things as they are: the Law loves a girl. It happens that she is, in your opinion, a bad girl. But *he* loves her and would like to marry her. He has first shown his respect for us, by marrying a wife whom we practically ordered him to take; but he expects, in return, that we should respect his individuality by accepting the choice he has made, of his own free will, to marry Agatha.

'To marry whom? Repeat the name you mentioned.'

'Agatha, I said Agatha Moudio.'

'Never, king; I tell you he will never marry her, or *I* shall disown him. What? That girl, who isn't satisfied with all she manages to do, but who also takes herself for a white woman . . . with dresses open everywhere, as if she wanted to show off her body to the whole world . . . If she becomes my son's wife she won't want to have a poor old woman like me anywhere near the Law . . . and she will do nothing with her hands . . . has a woman like that ever been known to work in the fields, or even to go and draw water for her husband? Tell me once more that the Law is going to marry such a creature, and I'll tell you once again that I shall disown him if he does so despite my opposition.'

'Woman,' said king Solomon finally, 'I don't want you to think that I'm going to encourage the Law to take a second wife, and still less to take that girl whom we all detest here. But I must warn you that in this kind of affair it isn't always possible to make one's own son see reason.'

And he left.

For my part, I went to demand some explanations from Agatha. She was in a vile temper.

'If you're like all the others in your village, if you think I'm a whore, I wonder what you come here for. You didn't want me when I offered myself. You preferred to listen to your mother and your village elders. Now, I intend to do as I please.'

It was clear: Agatha had stopped hoping that I would marry her one day. I went back home, and I asked Fanny not to bother any more about this matter with Maa Médi. I set about mending my cast-net, which was torn in several places. It would soon be the season of 'small fishing'; I had to be ready.

A month passed, during which my heart spoke no more of Agatha. Not at all. But this heart . . . it's when it doesn't speak that it shows itself.

One evening, when I was scarcely bothered any longer about what had become of her, Agatha Moudio came to see me, supposedly to ask the reason for my 'conclusive disappearance', and also to bring presents for my child. She offered Fanny some small things for the child and apologized for not coming before. 'The fact is that so few people like me in this village that I'm always obliged to worry about what they will say . . .'

That evening, Agatha told me about all sorts of plans which she intended to carry out. She was going off on a long journey, she was going to stay away a long time; in this way she was hoping to be forgotten in her village, by her parents, by our village, by everybody.

'You're not going to a very far-off country, I suppose?' I asked, interrupting her.

'Yes I am, she replied. 'I came to say good-bye, because I'm leaving tomorrow. I . . . I wanted your opinion . . . whether you want me to leave or not.'

I fell into the trap: I made it clear to Agatha that this departure upset me. I still wonder why it should have upset me, for to tell the truth, Agatha's recent goings-on had ended by putting me off her almost completely.

'No,' I said, 'don't leave your village. You know your father will be out of prison soon. He would be very unhappy to find you gone when he got back.'

'My father? Oh, it's all the same to him whether he finds me there or not, of that I'm well aware. If he loves me as much on his return as he did before he left, I don't see how my absence could spoil his pleasure in returning home. *That* wouldn't make me hesitate for a moment. What matters to me, at this moment, is the opinion of somebody much more important than my father. So, make up your mind . . . shall I leave tomorrow?'

I understood. How could I fail to understand? Agatha was in the process of making me a real declaration. Fanny winked; she had understood too. I saw her look, and it meant, quite clearly, 'Come on now, why let slip such a chance? Be reasonable; a woman who comes and asks you to take her, make no mistake, is a woman dying of love for you.'

I understood and turned to Agatha.

'Listen,' I told her, 'Maa Médi won't hear of our marriage, and nobody in our village would agree with me if I submitted my plan for general approval. Nobody, except perhaps king Solomon. Not even he holds you in very high esteem, but he is reasonable; and, in any case, I've told him everything. He knows everything there has been between you and me. Apart from him, there's Fanny. She wishes you no harm, quite the reverse. That makes two of us who don't want you to go off on your travels tomorrow, or even the day after.'

'Yes, it's true,' said Fanny. 'If the others didn't have to be considered, you know, you could come and live here whenever you like. But you really mustn't leave.'

Then Fanny turned back to her little Adela, and again began to sing a lullaby to send her to sleep. It was beginning to get late.

'Thank you,' said Agatha. Then she went away.

That very night, Mother Evil-Eye went to Maa Médi, and told her all she had seen – she saw everything in our village – pointed out to her that strange things were happening, and promised to stay on her guard. Then she went home, promising herself secretly that if 'their son' amused himself by doing 'such a thing' to them, she 'would cut the thread of pregnancy in his two wives'.

Only the calm night heard the low threats of Mother Evil-Eye.

10

In prison, Dooh had learned an honest trade. On his release, he set up in business on his own. He became a hairdresser, to the delight of our village and the district. He also took to drinking, 'to make the time pass more quickly' when the young men weren't particularly anxious to be made handsome.

The fine weather had returned with the passage of time. Dooh operated in the open air. He would sit on a huge, empty wooden box, under a mango tree, and there he patiently waited for custom. It was good to wait while drinking palm-wine. Dooh was doing just that one morning when a man came up to him:

'Cut my hair,' he ordered; 'I've heard about you; it seems that you do it very well.'

And the man sat down without waiting to be asked.

Dooh picked up a big stone, and with it he broke an empty beer bottle. Then he immediately knelt down around the pieces, as if to excuse himself for what he had just done. If the bottle had been full, he wouldn't have broken it. Oh, certainly not.

'You see,' said Dooh to his customer, 'you see, people who have nothing inside are like this bottle. They hardly deserve to be treated any better.'

'You are quite right,' replied the other. 'The earth is full to bursting with people with nothing inside.'

'You know, I'm not talking about hungry people ... what I'm saying is that stupid people don't deserve to live. What do you think?'

'You are right,' agreed the customer.

You have to agree with your hairdresser, up to the moment when he is ready to perform the miracle which transforms your head. Dooh, satisfied with the reply, whistled a tune, and chose a sharp piece of glass, uniformly curved. He thought it would serve his purpose. Then he approached his customer's neck, looked, and bent down to have a better look.

'Are *you* intelligent?'

'Certainly I'm intelligent,' said the customer. 'Do you think I should have come to find *you* if I weren't intelligent enough to realize that you're the best hairdresser in the region?'

'Oh, that, of course you're right. How stupid I am. Everybody knows I'm the best hairdresser around here. And then, if everybody doesn't know it yet, well, too bad, everybody will know one day. What do you bet?'

'Nothing, nothing at all, because I'm sure I'd lose.'

You couldn't deny it, this was the kind of customer that Dooh liked, the customer who always agreed with him. Out of the question, that being the case, to give him a bad cut. But the air smelled of palm-wine.

'Would you like a drop?' Dooh offered, stretching out his arm behind the box to bring out an enormous calabash.

He uncorked it, drank several mouthfuls, and then handed it to his customer. He also drank, unwilling to put down the calabash. 'It's good, brother, it's good . . .'

Then, the piece of broken bottle began to do its work on the customer's neck, gradually tracing the demarcation line between the head and the rest of the body. Dooh was pleased with his work. He went on whistling while he worked. Then he suddenly remembered that he had once attended the village school. There, he had learnt, in detail, the whole of the Old Testament, in the Douala tongue. Then he began to recite how Joshua won the battle of Jericho:

'... Then, the Israelites began blowing their trumpets and the walls of the town began to tremble ... to tremble, brother, until they collapsed ...'

The customer didn't understand where the passage came from:

'What are the Israelites doing behind my head?' he asked.

The hairdresser stopped short in his task:

'What,' he asked the ignorant one, '*you* ask me such a question? Don't you know ancient history? Don't you know the story of our ancestors?'

'But, tell me, what did they do then, our ancestors?'

'What did they do? What a question ... don't you know that they were condemned by God to wander in the desert for forty days and forty nights?'

'Ah? ...'

'Yes, yes ... for forty days and forty nights. It's a lot don't you think? No, I'm wrong. It was the flood which lasted forty days and forty nights. The Israelites wandered in the desert for forty years. And you know, real full years, such as we don't have any more these days ...'

'But what had they done then, to be condemned to that?'

'Nothing, really. Only God wasn't pleased with them, because they had disobeyed him. Then Moses went to beg the Pharaoh to let his people go.'

'Whose people?'

'God's people, for goodness' sake. You *are* stupid. You are like an empty bottle. You have nothing inside; you don't even deserve a good haircut. Don't you understand what I'm saying? I'm talking of God's people, of course ...'

'Oh ...'

'What, oh?'

'You're hurting me.'

'Oh, you're too sensitive, you are. It's the first time I've scratched you since we started, and you shriek as if I'd burnt your neck.'

A thread of blood ran gently down from the 'scratch'. Dooh stopped it in passing and continued to shave the hair on the rest of the neck. He had taken a bit more palm-wine than usual, and he went on with his extraordinary story of 'our ancestors the Israelites':

'Then, the Pharaoh collected the whole village round a big fire. There was a palaver for three days and three nights. And Moses brought a big snake which frightened everybody. But the Pharaoh had a heart of stone, and he wouldn't let the Israelites go. Then Moses called down a rainbow, and the rainbow spoke to the Pharaoh. But the Pharaoh had the rainbow's head cut off. Immediately, it grew dark, the Pharaoh's people were all blinded while Moses' men could see as clearly as in broad daylight. That's how they were able to get away ... ffft ... ffft ... ffft. Get up, that's it, I've finished. You look fine now. You can go and visit any woman; none of them will refuse you. And listen, when you are crowned with success, remember that it was I, Dooh, who made you handsome as you are now. Now pay me, and be off. I tell you that if you meet a woman on your way, and she refuses to look at your angelic head, you have only to come back and tell me and I will personally look into the matter . . . you can even go across the road. There's one there who won't resist you, shaped as you are . . .'

'Across the road? What is across the road?'

'Pay me first, it's one franc fifty. Can't you understand my way of speaking? It's obvious you've drunk all my wine. I tell you there's a woman opposite . . . yes, in that house there. She's everybody's wife. She belongs to everybody. Have you a little money? Yes? Then, you can go.'

The man paid fifty cents after a lot of bargaining. Then he went off 'across the road', while another customer was settling down on the packing-case, ready to submit to Dooh's cutting.

Now, 'across the road' was my house. That is why I was

astonished to see a man come in whom I didn't know, who was clearly almost drunk, and who, supposing that I was waiting (my turn, perhaps) said to me, without the least embarrassment:

'Brother, I've come too. Where is she then?'

'Who?' I asked.

'The woman,' said the man, his eyes sparkling with palm-wine and barely concealed desire. 'Yes,' he insisted, 'the woman. Brother hairdresser down there told me to come "across the road", if I had a little money. He said that here . . .'

I seized the man by the scruff of his neck, without giving him time to finish, and threw him out like a sack. Before he could get up I punched him in the face, and ordered him to go back home immediately, which he did without looking back. There were already a few people there, to see what was happening; but as far as I was concerned, I went straight to Dooh's hairdressing salon.

'You keep on playing tricks on me, Dooh, though I've warned you it would cost you dear one day. I think that day has now come, unfortunately for you.'

I grabbed him and hit him in a way that he'll remember till the end of his days, at least I hope so, for I wouldn't want him to forget the punishment he received at my hands that day, and start again one day to tell everybody that I've married a whore. The inhabitants of the village intervened in time, just as I was busy making the impudent Dooh bite the dust. Some women started begging me not to kill him, for he was a brother and 'if your brother does you wrong, you must forgive him'. This provided a good reason for me to cool down . . . in fact, thanks to Dooh's foolishness, which had given me a chance to prove to everybody that I was still the strongest chap around, I had once again gathered around me people, men and women who had been doing their utmost to send me to Coventry for some two months past.

You will easily understand what had happened if you realize that even at this moment, when I was the object of the unwilling admiration of them all, Maa Médi didn't appear; she who used to rush out first of them all whenever I put on a show of strength. For almost two months I had been living alone, with my two wives and Fanny's child. I went alone to the fishing, in spite of king Solomon's personal intervention, when at great length he begged my comrades to keep me in their crew. 'We are fond of the Law,' they had replied, 'but when he finds it amusing to marry a woman who is a disgrace to our community, then we are no longer on his side ...' The break had occurred about a week after the evening when Agatha had come to visit us and had spoken so frankly, a visit which had, you will remember, attracted the attention of Mother Evil-Eye. In fact, shortly after that evening, she returned one night, accompanied by one of her aunts. 'It was to my house that Agatha came when she visited the town,' the aunt had told us. Each of them was carrying a case, a heavy case. They had settled down and had themselves decided that Agatha would not return to her village. 'She is your wife from tonight,' Agatha's aunt had told me, 'and I wish you happiness throughout your life. I know that everything will be all right with Fanny, won't it?' Fanny didn't reply, but I knew she was not against my marriage to Agatha. She had been very kind and the very next day she had built a hearth for Agatha like the one my mother had prepared for her. My mother? She came to see me the next morning, together with Mother Evil-Eye:

'I have come to see you and speak to you in the presence of someone who will be my witness even after my death. You have refused to heed my advice, and you have taken this girl. Stay with her and I hope you may never regret it. As for me, I know that this little white wife you have just married will lead you a dance, till you can't tell white from black. Wait; but when you are in trouble, don't come to me; I want to be left in peace . . . whether I die of poverty or grief, or whether I go on living in spite of everything, I want you to leave me in peace. And listen carefully to what I'm saying; don't expect to see me here any more. Never again.'

And the two women had left without letting me get in a word. Since then, we had been living together, the four of us, my two wives, 'my daughter', and I, and the whole village avoided us as much as possible. Actually, king Solomon, who was very fond of me and understood me fairly well, would never leave me completely in the cold; but since the imprisonment of Chief Mbaka, he was acting Chief of the village, and obviously, he couldn't show everybody, openly, that he forgave me for marrying Agatha Moudio. We had now been living like that for two months. And, as if in reaction to the harsh way in which people in the village treated us and looked on us, we made an effort to create in our home a harmony which, alas, we could never recapture later. During this period, Agatha behaved in a manner of which nobody believed her capable. She went to get water at the fountain, in spite of all the double-edged remarks the other women threw at her every time she went there. She did the cooking properly, she, whom Maa Médi had called a grand lady. Fanny, for her part, had matured a lot; she had become a real woman, and, as my mother had once said, 'ready to give me children'. I must give her a breather, I told myself, thinking of her comparatively recent confinement. As for little Adela, she was beginning to come to life, and she became more and more interesting as the days went by.

Naturally my house, originally designed for a single person, soon proved too small for the four of us. So I set myself to work building other houses: one for Fanny, another for Agatha. And I had been busy at this job when that imbecile Dooh had made me so furious, as I was telling you a minute ago.

And now, there I was, in the middle of all the villagers who had come, some to watch me 'kill' Dooh, others to admire me from head to foot, and others to beg me not to 'do that'. And so Dooh, who had it in for Agatha not only because she had become my wife, but also because he remained convinced that she had shopped him, Dooh, I say, merely succeeded, without intending to do so, in breaking the ice which had thickened for nearly two months between my people and me. I saw some smiles when, negligently, I dropped the idiot on the ground and threw him a look of profound contempt. These smiles meant that they appreciated my way of 'forgiving a brother who had done me wrong'. And then, what can you really do with a man who gets drunk on palm-wine at ten in the morning?

From that day on, the whole village showed clemency towards me, and especially towards Agatha. After all, she wasn't turning out as bad as they had expected at the start. And then, even if they disapproved of her premarital adventures, that was already in the past, wasn't it? Come on now, that's all over . . . and then, what sort of way is this to receive a stranger in our community? It didn't look good.

The only people who wouldn't forgive Agatha for having 'chased me till she got me', were still Maa Médi and Mother Evil-Eye. In spite of that, life became bearable for us in the village and I could now boast of being one of the upholders of an ancestral tradition which, alas, comes under bitter attack these days: polygamy.

It would take too long to relate in detail what went on in our triple household, and I reserve the right to be silent on many points, because I can imagine the amused smile with which you would prepare to listen to my story. I don't consider that situation simply as something amusing . . . I wouldn't want, either, to bore you with the details of the life my two wives led me from the day when the village having for all practical purposes accepted my second marriage, they could no longer see a reason for the unity which had until then been perfect. Each of them now lived in her own house; each of them could, if she wished and felt energetic enough, prepare her own meal, in her own house, always having in mind, of course, their common husband. This they soon decided to do. One day, when I had left for a spell on the high seas, Agatha and Fanny found a reason to quarrel. 'My son, you've never seen anything like it,' king Solomon told me on my return. I called them into my house, to ask what had happened:

'It was Fanny who started it,' Agatha hastened to say.

'What? *I* started it? Because I presumed to point out that you did nothing in the house? Because I refuse to be your slave?'

'You hear? She says I did nothing, when it was I who was preparing food for you. I should say it was *you* who took *me* for your slave.'

'You were preparing food? You can talk: a woman who prepares food without going to fetch water herself but waits for somebody else to do it for her, wouldn't you say she thinks of herself as a queen and everybody else as her slaves?'

'Just listen to that ... while you were fetching water, wasn't I sweeping the house?'

'What house, what house? Did I find my house swept?'

This argument, at first sight merely banal and vulgar, went on in front of me for a long time. When two women have things to say to each other, you must let them speak freely, even if you are the husband of both of them. These insignificant things can be very important. In this case, they led to the complete separation of my two wives. To say that this made me unhappy would be to lie too glibly. On the contrary, the unity of these two women, at the beginning, had rather scared me. For I remembered very well what had happened with Etoka, when his two wives began to get on too well together. Etoka suffered a lot. Just imagine, the two women organized nights out without telling him, and they both went off to visit young men while their old husband slept alone in his bed, after spending half the night looking for them everywhere in the village, literally going from door to door. People made fun of Etoka: 'When he had plenty of money,' said one, 'I gave him the following advice: "Etoka, my brother, now that you have some money put by, don't do anything stupid. Buy a lot of canoes, you can hire them out to fishermen or transporters and that will bring in money." That's what I told Etoka, and I was speaking as I would have spoken to a blood brother. But he didn't listen to me. He preferred to take several wives. Look at him now . . .' And then another added: 'Now he's well off, with his two wives,' and burst out laughing. 'An old man like that,' said yet another mocker, 'he thinks he's still a young man . . . it amuses him to marry wives thirty years younger than himself, and he thinks he'll be able to keep them at home. I tell you he's still got it coming to him . . .'

Etoka was the laughing-stock of the whole district, with his two wives 'who rarely slept at home'. So I didn't want to have to join him one day, with wives who got on too well together. The universal tactics of polygamy are based on a carefully fostered disunity between the wives. Remember this, if ever one day . . . That is why, at heart, I was quite pleased to see things taking a turn more convenient for me. I was even better pleased to see that in this argument, which might have seemed quite harmless, there had crept in an element which could be sure to perpetuate the growing disharmony; to be precise, Fanny had discovered that her rival, Agatha, was 'much older' than her. That was not really correct since, as you know, there was not more than four or five years' difference in their ages. But it was quite enough to give Fanny the sweetly sparkling air of a young girl speaking to 'an older woman', as she said. Just see how she had twisted the facts, and presented them with a good measure of hypocrisy in her simplicity: 'I don't understand,' she said in surprised tones, 'I have the same husband as my aunt who came to join me here and I . . .'

'What? You call me your aunt? Because you want to remind everybody that I'm older than you? Why don't you go and shout in the street that I brought you into the world? And that I'm the grandmother of an illegitimate child?'

You see, it was now vicious enough to make me safe. I thanked my stars, and didn't worry any more at all when I had to be away for a whole month, as my job required. But it was when I got back from fishing that you should have seen what went on in our home. Each of my wives expected me to go to her house before I went to visit her rival. That made me seriously regret, now and then, that I couldn't be two people.

It was when I came back from fishing one day that I provoked the 'final departure' of Agatha. During my absence the two women had had another violent quarrel: 'My son, you never saw anything like it, they almost came to blows,' king Solomon reported to me.

'What's happened this time?' I asked the two ladies.

'Agatha said that the next time you buy me a dress without giving her one like it, she'll go.'

'Yes, that's right,' said Agatha. 'That's right; and what did you answer?'

'I said that if you leave, you might as well leave for good, for my husband won't come and ask you to return . . .'

'Your husband, your husband . . . do you hear? That's what makes me angry. Your husband . . . as if he were yours and yours alone. You're nothing but a little egoist and you think of nobody but yourself. Your forget that I knew the Law before you did, and that if I had wanted to, I could have come here before you did . . . and then you would certainly never have set foot in the place.'

'Don't talk so much, "elder aunt", I'm, not allowed to argue with you. Simply let time pass and the future will decide . . .'

Agatha almost slapped Fanny's face to 'punish her for her insolence'. I intervened in time and there was no fight. Each of them went back to her house, certain that I should come to her before going to the other. How can a man split himself in two and go at the same time to visit two wives? I could find no solution to this serious problem. I went first . . . to Fanny's, on the pretext that I wanted to see little Adela. This inevitably made Agatha lose her bet that I would go to her before going to Fanny's. What a business . . . Agatha went mad with rage. She even came to Fanny's house.

It's odd, and it seems odder and odder when I think of it now: where once I would have accepted almost any humiliation in my ardent desire to marry Agatha, she now seemed to me very little different from any other woman . . . and I had even gone to Fanny's before going to her, when I should have supported her in her proud claim to have 'known me first'.

She came in like a whirlwind:

'I understand,' she said, 'you come and see your wife before coming to me. You don't come to me first, because *I* don't have a child to show you. Very well, I'll give you a child too. But first . . . you will come and make amends for the way you have insulted me . . . you will come yourself and make amends at my aunt's. And if you don't come to fetch me back, I shall stay there. In that way, there will be peace of mind for everybody in this village.'

She ran out. I tried to catch her, but she was already in the street. In the compound, I saw Maa Médi. She had come out because she had heard the noise. She saw me running to try to catch Agatha. She gave a bitter smile, which spoke volumes. She didn't speak to me but I knew what she was thinking: 'My poor boy, it's not finished yet, the trouble you'll have with this hell-cat that you took in spite of my formal prohibition. I told you, she'll lead you a fine dance . . .' She went back into her house and shut the door. I was ashamed, and that evening I had no appetite. Fanny, for her part, didn't spare me:

'That doesn't surprise me,' she said nastily when I could hardly eat, 'your wife, your real wife, has gone, and you have lost your appetite, haven't you? *I* count for nothing here . . .'

'How awful they are,' I thought; 'horrible, both of them.'

I decided that I would not go and fetch Agatha back. She could wait at her aunt's as long as she liked, but I wouldn't go and beg her to come back to us. Naturally, when the village people heard that the beautiful Agatha had gone away 'to her aunt's in the town', they had a good gloat over this news that had fallen from heaven to keep the village gossips going. For them, their forecasts were coming true, exactly as they had predicted. For them, Agatha couldn't be a wife to keep at home: 'She was born to live outside', they would say, in spite of the propriety of her behaviour at the beginning of her stay in our village. Now, her flight merely confirmed what people said, especially as she had left my house, not for her own village nearby, but for the town where her aunt lived, which, in their eyes, was merely a pretext. They went further, informing me that from time to time, when I was away, Agatha used to go off to the town. This information, on top of everything else, didn't please me much, for Agatha herself had never told me that she went to the town when I wasn't there. But I thought the whole thing out like a reasonable man; then I told myself that these rumours were hardly likely to present Agatha in a favourable light, whatever the facts were, taking into account what she had been before her marriage, and also the lack of enthusiasm with which she had been received in the village. Moreover, I reasoned that if Agatha went out in my absence, Fanny wouldn't have failed to let me know, even if only during one of the arguments which you have heard yourselves. I therefore purely and simply rejected the growing rumours, and I stayed peacefully at home working before going off fishing again.

No matter. The big news, day and night, in the village, was Agatha's departure. Everybody offered his own version of the story, and there were soon so many versions that nobody knew what to believe. Fortunately, other events soon came to fill the front page of our spoken newspaper.

There was first the birth of Endalé's daughter. This was much talked about, for you will remember that Endalé's husband had already been deported when she had found a way of conceiving a child. We all knew Endalé's husband. We knew what a violent temper he had and we were wondering, not without some anxiety, what fate was in store on his return for Endalé, who had deceived him. Meanwhile the baby prospered and was the sun of our village.

Uncle Big-Heart's house produced another subject of conversation. It had in fact just been finished. King Solomon had not built it all alone. He had combined with two other stone-masons, engaged by my uncle, some months after the 'affair' when everybody had sent him to Coventry and the king himself had abruptly decided that he wouldn't work again for 'that evil sorcerer'. Today, uncle Big-Heart's house was a sight to be seen: it was beautiful, whitewashed, with the basement creosoted, its roof of corrugated iron shining in the sun. It gave our village a stylish and prosperous appearance, which struck strangers at first glance. In the end, we were all proud of it: it was our monument. Uncle Big-Heart gave a big party, and we ate, and drank, and danced, and laughed. 'When the others are back,' said uncle Big-Heart, transported with joy, 'there will be a still bigger party.' There was no need to predict this; for how could we have welcomed 'the others' on their return from Mokolo without showing our joy, after those four long years of separation? In any case, their return wasn't very far off now. What joy we had to look forward to . . .

11

As for Agatha, she returned to the village some two weeks after her flight, one evening. She returned without letting anybody know. Agatha was like that. I was preparing to leave the next morning with my mates for the fishing grounds in the estuary. It was the height of the season.

Agatha came back, more reasonable than on the occasion of her noisy departure that other evening. She came to apologize to me, and surprised me by doing the same to Fanny. 'What a good nature,' I said to myself. It was really difficult to know where to start with that woman . . . 'We'll talk about all that later, when I get back,' I answered. And the next morning, I left to breathe the sea air and the wind laden with spray.

'Is it true that Agatha came back last night?' Ekéké asked me.

'Who told you?' I countered.

I didn't want to start on this chapter of my life story with my cousin, for he had shown himself no better than the others towards me when more or less fantastic versions of Agatha's flight had begun to spread through the village street.

'Who told me? I am a child of this village, what do you

think? I know everything that happens. And then, the women know everything, too.'

'Oh good, I understand: your wife went to get water at the fountain this morning . . .'

I said this with a grain of malice in my voice, for you are well aware that my cousin Ekéké was not yet married.

'Don't get angry, brother *La Loi*,' he said; 'if your wife has returned, we all share your joy, don't we?'

The others in the canoe agreed, claiming that I had no right to keep from them a piece of news which concerned them. They seemed sincere. So the friendly atmosphere was maintained and it was I who had to apologize to them for my morning bad temper:

'You know,' I told Ekéké, 'when you are married, you will understand how it is; you will gradually lose your natural gaiety.'

'Especially if you have two wives at home,' said Eyango. 'Two wives at home, brother, will be the death of you sooner or later.'

'I wonder where I could possibly get the idea of marrying more than one wife. Life with just one must be difficult enough.'

There were three bachelors in the crew and three of us were married men; I was the only one who had two wives.

'I don't see what's so difficult about marriage for two,' continued Eboumbou. 'Since I've been married, I don't see much change from what I was before.'

'*You* don't see,' said Eyango, 'but *we* see the difference clearly: you work much harder nowadays than you did before.'

Laughter spread from stem to stern, while the paddles momentarily ceased from dipping in the river water.

'Yes, it's true, brother,' insisted Eyango. 'Don't get annoyed, but remember how many fishing trips you took part in each year, when you were still a bachelor. You were missing three quarters of the time; and what did you live on? It's true you weren't a beggar, but you often went for a meal to your uncle's, or your aunt's, or one friend or another . . . without it costing you a penny, just like the old men. Whereas now, you come with us every time we go out; and you have money to provide for your needs, and those of your wife.'

'That's to say, if I understand correctly, that's to say that marriage forces a man to work? But why, then,' said Eboumbou, 'are you against the idea of several wives?'

'That's a good question you've just asked, brother,' I said.

'We're not against marriage with several wives,' Ekéké corrected. 'We couldn't deliberately go against a practice which was completely usual with our ancestors. For my part, I simply think it must be rather difficult these days to lead such a life without reckoning that it forces you to work even harder. Just think: to keep two or three wives.'

Today, time and mixing with people who 'know about life' have given my arguments a certain measure of 'civilization'. I consider work as good and useful. It is, I confess, an opinion which doesn't come naturally to a man. The natural tendency is to consider work, and not unreasonably, as simply something tiring. Such was my view of it at that time, and that is why I could so easily understand my cousin Ekéké's reflections. But if it is true that marriage makes a man do more and more work, and if one lays down once and for all that work is good, then one can do nothing but encourage men to marry as many wives as possible. And if there are, in this world, women who still believe that they were born to have their husbands to themselves, then everything must be done to bring them round to the opinion that marriage with a man at the centre of several wives is a matter of public utility.

My ancestors, by inventing polygamy, which was openly

accepted by all, thought of all the benefits to be got from it by modern societies. Today I hear men and women who blame them for this initiative, and yet I see no human society, however highly civilized, where the principles of my ancestors are not more or less faithfully applied. Monogamy exists nowhere in the world, and I am proud to think that in our humble village, unknown by the great societies of the rest of the world, it had been far from the rule for a very long time. It is true that those who invented polygamy, in those happy days when my ancestors had little idea of time, were not thinking of working harder, and this was natural: time and work are such closely connected concepts that one cannot, without risk of error, think of one dissociated from the other. Then, time didn't exist, or if it did, it had the value of a sunny day, to which corresponded the work necessary for the needs of the day. It is modern times which have introduced, as a result of polygamy, an increase in the necessity to work for men . . .

We were rowing gently towards the estuary of the Wouri. A tropical morning, hot and humid at the same time; no comparison with the so-called temperate countries. And there was my cousin Ekéké – it's true he had been to school, and had learned quite a few things – there he was talking to *us* and using terms which I was to meet again only later on, in the mouths of people 'who know about life', or 'who lived like Europeans', as you will.

'. . . Maintaining two or three wives . . .' he was saying.

'It's not a matter of maintaining them,' said Eboumbou to my cousin, 'it's simply a matter of giving them a chance to lead a woman's life: to be in a home, to produce children for the necessary continuation of the human race, to bring them up in the best possible way. What is a woman, according to you? A wreck, trailing around the streets, or a stake at the corner of a house, trying to catch any man passing by? No, that's not what *I* call a woman. And you know, that wouldn't happen if each man married several wives. That's why, brother *La Loi*, I congratulate you on not having left Agatha on the path on which she had almost set out and on having stood up to us when we expressed our disapproval of your marriage with her.'

As confessions go, I said to myself, there's one that surprises me.

'Thank you,' I replied to Eboumbou. 'But I wonder why you didn't indicate at the time that you agreed with me?'

'You know,' he told me, 'in an affair like that you have to act like everybody else. It was still a burning question; how could I involve myself, when everybody was against you? Simply let me tell you that personally, I never disapproved.'

It was the first time I had received such a frank admission. I told myself that it certainly wouldn't be the last, provided that Agatha didn't begin again and disappoint all my comrades who, in their heart of hearts, agreed with my marrying her, in spite of appearances.

When we returned from fishing, great news awaited us on the bank: a letter had come from Mokolo, announcing that the prisoners had only about six months left to spend in exile. Now, everybody was counting the days, one after the other. 'We shall see them again, we shall see them again, those who left one morning, in handcuffs, and who didn't come back . . .' During their absence, king Solomon had written to them from time to time, to keep them informed of what was happening in our villages. We could not be certain that they had ever received these letters from the king; if they had, they were prepared for the . . . surprises which awaited them. Otherwise, we all feared that their homecoming might be a bit stormy.

I went home, and there I was surprised to find my two wives in perfect harmony. Then I remembered Agatha's gesture when she had gone to ask Fanny's pardon. And

Fanny, on her side, had admitted *her* mistakes. Now, apparently, they understood each other like two sisters. I felt reasonably pleased, for it was so hot that I should certainly have found it difficult to put up with a row on my return. That day, instead of each of them coming to report to me what her rival had been doing during my absence, instead of each of them pressing me to come to her house and have dinner with her before I set foot in her neighbour's, instead of all that, I was surprised to learn that we were all three going to eat together. 'What a change . . .' I thought. I was so pleased that I completely forgot Etoka's wives, who had started to get on so well together that their joint husband became the laughing-stock of the whole district. But there were more surprises to come: in fact, on the evening of the same day, Agatha came to see me in my room; she sat down on my bed without waiting to be asked, and announced calmly:

'You know, *La Loi*, I'm expecting a child.'

'What? What are you saying?' I asked, sitting down.

'I'm telling you you're going to be the father of a son.'

'How do you know it will be a boy?'

'Because I dreamed it would be a girl. When a woman dreams that she's expecting a girl, she's sure to have a boy. It always happened like that when my mother was expecting a child. She dreamed she would have a boy and she had a girl. Each time, the same thing happened.'

Agatha and I then had a long conversation, going over and clarifying the situation from the day when it had got progressively worse. Spare me these conversations between husband and wife. The most important thing in all that was, naturally, the news which Agatha had just given me. The very next morning I went to see king Solomon.

'Agatha is expecting a child, king. But sh . . . don't tell anybody.'

'That's good, and just in time, since her father will be

back soon. That will give him double pleasure: finding his daughter married, and having a child ... If, in addition, she has the bright idea of giving birth to a boy ... the whole village will be on your side, son, you'll see. I told you to look ahead and not behind. You see what I have always told you?'

King Solomon was getting excited.

'That's all very well,' I told him, 'but the fact remains that Maa Médi can't stand Agatha. If you could go and talk to her and tell her what's going to happen, it would no doubt be a good idea.'

'Certainly, it would be a good idea,' the king assured me.

He went to Maa Médi and spoke to her.

The result was immediate, and unexpected:

'She's expecting a child?' asked Maa Médi; 'a child for my son? A real child for my son? That changes everything. I should be wrong to stick to the position I have taken, now that the situation has changed. I am happy, king, I am happy.'

She ran out of her house and came to find me. There will never be anybody like this good woman in my life.

'Son,' she said to me, 'it's nothing, it's nothing, what you did to me. If it's the will of heaven that your disobedience should bring you happiness, it's not for me to go against it. I have only to submit, and I share your happiness. What did I say? All your happiness is mine too. From today, I place myself at your wife's disposal to help with the house-work; and from now on I consider her as my own daughter ... a child, a child, is always precious.'

I called Agatha, who was very pleased to learn that Maa Médi forgave her for having 'chased me until she got me'. They embraced. I was quite overcome. Fanny too had come to be present at the reconciliation. We were all very happy. I thanked Maa Médi and kissed her as in the days when I was still a little boy. Then I went to my room and brought her all

I had saved for her while she would have nothing to do with me and was refusing any financial help from me.

So, with a joyful heart, I was making a fresh start in life. And yet, this intense joy didn't in any way mean that it was all over and that I'd have no more worries. A pregnancy, in our village, was never simply the business of one person only. Maa Médi went straight to Mother Evil-Eye's, and spoke to her in a low voice:

'What? She's expecting a child, that girl? And since when is she expecting a child?'

'Since when? I have no idea . . . you could hardly expect king Solomon to tell me since when my daughter-in-law is expecting a child.'

'It needs looking into carefully,' said Mother Evil-Eye. 'You, Médi, it's too easy to get round you. And what if this chit has made up the story, just to get you on her side? Are you going to believe that, as if you had checked it? We must check the matter before saying anything at all, and especially before making it up with our son, the Law.'

'Listen, Eye, a child is not something you can invent. A pregnancy will always be obvious, if it's genuine. So why do you want to go and check now a fact we shall have plenty of time to analyse for months, a short time from now? I dont' see the need.'

'I insist, because I know from experience that one can't accept things like that. I know what I'm talking about. I have a kind of feeling that you can't believe all this story. Look Médi, doesn't it seem odd to you? A girl like her . . . she waits for her husband to return to tell him she's going to have a child. Does that seem altogether natural, to you?'

'What do you mean?'

'I mean that if she were expecting a child, she would have shouted it aloud through the whole village, so that everybody should know that, in spite of what's been said about her, she's not barren.'

'Oh, good, you reassure me.'

'What? I reassure you? When I tell you again that I myself am not happy with the course this story has taken, *you* tell me I reassure you? I tell you again that something must be done, to see if it's all true.'

Then they invited two other women, of the kind 'who never tell what they have in their hearts', which means that they can keep a secret. They told them what they had just learned, and, naturally, Mother Evil-Eye did her best to impress on them the need for care.

'My belief in such statements is limited, especially coming from a girl of her kind,' she confessed to them. 'Therefore it's our duty to "visit" Agatha.'

Maa Médi came in person to call her for this. They shut themselves up with her in a dark room, undressed her, and the examination began. In the darkness, they examined the surface of her abdomen in the greatest detail. 'I'm still wondering what they expected to see there,' Agatha was to tell me later. They asked no questions. They merely went, themselves, into the next room, to discuss in low voices each time one of them had 'discovered' something. Agatha couldn't understand the meaning of their whispers through the thin wall which separated the two rooms. 'A strange kind of examination,' Agatha thought. Nobody sounded her, nobody laid a finger on her. They must have had special eyes to check that there was indeed an embryo in this abdomen. Then they told Agatha to get dressed again, which she did immediately . . . 'If you knew how embarrassed I was . . .' She had good reason: four old women who come and look at the skin of your abdomen in the darkness of a room where only they can see clearly, and who then go off next door to whisper about what they've seen and not seen, what they think and don't think. At the end of the examination, three of the four faces came and told Agatha that it was over, 'for the moment, but there are other precautions to be taken'.

Three faces. The fourth, that of Mother Evil-Eye, remained enclosed in a scepticism which even the serenity of my wife herself couldn't shake. But that seemed to us normal, for it was very unusual, in our village, for opinion to be unanimous about a pregnant woman. The fact that Mother Evil-Eye continued to look askance at the fact that my second wife was going to have a child hardly surprised us: we knew that *that* lady was not at all pleased by the increase which had taken place in the population of our village in recent times. Remember Maa Médi's joy on the day when Mother Evil-Eye had called Fanny to 'bless' her, as we used to say with a smile. For it was unusual for the old witch to take anyone under her protection like that. 'My daughter,' she had told her, 'you will have many children . . .' and Fanny had started by giving me an illegitimate child.

'Too bad,' Maa Médi said to me, thinking of Mother Evil-Eye's bad temper, 'too bad, I'm sure it's not she who's right. And then, you can always make her happy, if you give her something.'

So it was that two days later, I had to go to Mother Evil-Eye's, to take her a little present: some tobacco, some cooking salt, a multi-coloured headscarf and an earthenware pipe. With all that, she could annul the effects of the spell which she had certainly cast on Agatha.

'Thank you, thank you, son,' she said to me. 'You are still the good little boy that we have always known. I'm not angry with you any more, or with your wife Agatha either. But last night, I dreamed of her. You will have to send for somebody to examine her, for I have a feeling she's made a bad start . . .'

'Send for somebody? It's serious then?'

'Perhaps not, but I don't know which herb can put her right.'

'Put her right? It's serious then? Mother Eye, tell me, you know she is expecting a boy . . .'

'Be silent, son. Who told you she's expecting a boy? And then, who told you to say such things out loud? Go on, you, you're a man, this kind of thing doesn't concern you. We others must take care of it.'

We sent for 'somebody' and the fetishist quickly found the magic herb which broke the spell which had fallen on Agatha, for precisely what reason, I don't know.

However, in spite of all that, Mother Evil-Eye wouldn't give up her reservations concerning my wife's pregnancy. There are people like that with a fixed idea which they cherish until the day when it's proved true or false. This old witch with four eyes must definitely have been thinking of something difficult to put into words. Her attitude created a pessimistic atmosphere which gradually enveloped me, making me apprehensive during the months which followed, while, however, the dimensions of Agatha's abdomen, taking hitherto unknown proportions, clearly showed that my wife was expecting a child. 'What's the matter with her, what's the matter with her then?' each of us wondered. And as nobody managed to discover what was the matter with Mother Evil-Eye, I ended by telling myself that it was quite possible that nothing at all was the matter, and little by little I stopped worrying about her.

Months passed, during which time Maa Médi remained literally at Agatha's service, to such an extent that one day Fanny found it necessary to point out that when *she* was pregnant my mother had not helped her as much. Women always see the good which has not been done them. As if more help from my mother could have prevented Fanny from giving me an illegitimate child . . .

The day when a telegram arrived from Yaoundé telling us that the exiles had already arrived there, and that all that remained now was for them to take the train to come down to Douala, everybody began getting ready for their imminent arrival. Two days later, we all went to the town, to the station, to meet the train coming from the capital. The return of the prisoners was moving. The joy of meeting again was unbounded, but at the same time, there was no less profound sorrow at finding that the number of our men had decreased since their departure for the distant regions of North Cameroun. Endalé was there, her heart beating. What would her husband say when he came home? She was not the only one who had 'won' a child while losing a husband for a time, but she was the most afraid, being well aware of her husband's violent nature. When I say she had lost him for a time . . . fate, for its part, had not interpreted it so.

'He died at Mokolo,' they told us.

There were still more tears when we were told that Chief Mbaka, as well as Agatha's paternal uncle, had also died there.

'If we are still alive,' said Eya, the husband of Mother Evil-Eye, 'I'm still wondering how it comes about. If you knew what ill-treatment they subjected us to up there . . . for four endless years . . .'

They revealed that they had never received a single one of king Solomon's letters. So, when we returned to our respective villages, the first thing we did was to gather together, so as to bring the new arrivals up to date about what had happened in their absence. I need hardly say that it took some time to make these men accept that uncle Big-Heart, who had 'caused their imprisonment', was no longer banned from our midst. But my uncle had admitted his mistakes and king Solomon, as well as the chief of Agatha's village, showed themselves to be talented advocates. The men finally reached complete agreement, and our community prepared to carry out the duties which the present situation required.

'Nobody shall go fishing tomorrow,' king Solomon decreed. 'No woman shall go to work in the fields tomorrow,' he added. 'Tomorrow is a day of meditation: we shall think of our brothers who died in exile.'

And the next day was a day of mourning. The women wept in the village square. They wept and sang laments and danced to funereal rhythms. The men shut themselves up in some of their houses, smoking pipes, drinking palm-wine, and singing the lament for those who never return to their country: 'You march, you march ceaselessly, you do not return, oh my brother, you do not return. You go away without looking back, and you do not return, oh my brother, I see that you do not return. Who lied to you and told you one should leave like that? Who taught you to march like that? When a man marches, he turns round from time to time to see those he has left behind him, those who are dear to him. You, you march ceaselessly, you do not turn back. Who lied to you and told you one leaves one's friends like that? Tell me: who lied to you and told you that one leaves one's brothers thus?'

The next day was peaceful. Some women continued to weep, but the men had gradually returned to their everyday occupations. For the moment, in any case, the main thing was to prepare the feast for the return of the prisoners. It would take place the following Sunday. We had three days before us. Three days during which I had other duties to perform. Of course, you remember the circumstances in which I had finally married Agatha Moudio. You know how she had come of her own accord to settle in my house, at a time when I no longer expected her, what's more. Agatha was, as she said herself, a 'free girl'. 'My father? He doesn't bother about me': that's what she had told me on that day when, after throwing a handful of cooking salt on the fire she had taken advantage of the rain to stay with me. You remember. And when she came to my house on another evening, with her two heavy cases and accompanied by her aunt, she got married in the manner of a girl who had complete liberty of movement and action. However, as soon as Moudio was back, and as soon as he learned that his daughter was married, he lost no time in coming to see me, to wish me 'a good marriage with his daughter', and to ask me what I intended to do in the future. That simply meant that I must view the future with a certain number of bottles and presents for my father-in-law:

'What? You take my daughter and I haven't even drunk a drop of "water"?' Moudio asked me.

So it came about that on the same day I bought a long, wide cloth, as well as two bottles of Scotch water, of the famous Johnny Walker brand. In the evening, I called king Solomon, and we went together to see Moudio. We found all his village gathered in his house, listening to his account of the imprisonment. 'My brothers, I wouldn't wish you ever to go up there. Do all that you want to do here, but if one day the white man comes and asks if you want to go to Mokolo, even if it's to become the richest man on earth, tell him: "No, sir, *I* don't want to go up there." If you accept, my brothers, you're going to your death . . .' Moudio drank a swig of gin, good, clear gin, which the people of his village had bought to celebrate his return. Then he went on: 'The road, to get to those northern parts, is in itself a torture. You can't imagine: a road which goes uphill, with endless bends, and which when you get to the top allows you to see the distance you have travelled. It's at that moment that you realize with horror that you've escaped from the jaws of death. All the time like that. Cliffs, ravines . . . and then, you get to a river, swollen immeasurably by the winter rains, and you wonder how you are going to get across without being carried away by the current, which is so fast that oxen and horses are drowned and die . . .'

'It's the Red Sea,' said somebody, 'our brother has seen the Red Sea in the days of the Pharaoh.'

'No, brother,' said Moudio. 'That sea wasn't at all red.

It's called the Benue. It goes as far as the "English zone" and then into the sea . . .'

'To the sea? You say the sea? Where we go fishing?'
'Yes, the same sea.'

'But then, that means that you weren't very far from home . . . Mokolo wasn't very far away then . . .'

'I'm talking about the sea, but I didn't say that Mokolo was in that direction. And you know, if I could have thrown myself in the water and swum to the sea, I would certainly have preferred it to the terrible times I had in that prison. And then, the heat . . . the heat which burns your throat . . . oh, give me something to drink, in revenge.'

He was given another glass of gin, drank some, and went on telling the story of this cursed prison.

'All that . . .' he said, 'because of a sorcerer belonging to those people . . . and then I come back, and I'm told it's one of their sons who has taken Agatha away from me . . . the Law, come here?'

He shouted so loud that those people who didn't know that king Solomon and I had come in were terrified, thinking that Moudio had perhaps gone mad. We approached with our gifts, and the king spoke to offer the presents.

'My son', said the king, 'my son didn't take your daughter without your permission, as if he didn't know that you are Agatha's father. He was merely waiting for you to come back to give you this little present. Take this cloth, and forget the bad time you've been through. And then, here's a little "water" to quench your thirst. Don't refuse.'

Refuse? How the devil could he refuse? Who could refuse to welcome to his house the man in the top hat, striding jauntily, holding his long stick, on the square bottle from Scotland? Moudio took the two bottles of alcohol, opened one immediately, and shed a few drops on the ground, saying: 'Liquor, it's a long time since I saw you; so when I drink you, I don't want you to give me headaches.' And he poured himself out a full glass; and the others came too with their glasses, asking for their first ration of whisky. I had won the day. I knew that henceforward, nobody in this village would refuse to accept me as Agatha's husband. It was strange, in any case, that they had all let me do as I wished, without the slightest protest, when I had 'taken their daughter'.

It's true that Agatha had formerly forbidden me to receive anybody who might come from her village and ask for a present on the grounds that I had married 'his' daughter. 'They have never done anything for me,' she had told me, 'so I consider that my marriage is no concern of theirs and they have no right to gain from it.' And as they were reproaching themselves for never having done anything for Agatha, they wisely stayed away. Nobody came to claim the traditional 'bottle'. Of course, the evil tongues in our village provided an explanation for this which tended rather to make me angry than to show how honest and unselfish Agatha's relations were: 'Come and claim the bottle! They wouldn't dare! They know very well that their daughter would probably never have had a husband if one of our men hadn't turned up. The Law's doing them a service, by taking this fallen girl.' So, when Moudio, on his return, came and asked for 'a drop of water', I regarded this as a real relief for me, rather than as a duty to be carried out. There was now proof that I was not marrying 'a girl who belonged to nobody', as our people had been only too ready to say. I was happy to go and offer him the gifts which king Solomon and I had brought. It's true that my father-in-law went further than I had expected, for he and his people obliged me, in addition, to contribute money to the preparation of the festivities which they were organizing to celebrate his return to his birthplace. And when they knew I would do so, these good people of Bonakamé folded their arms, telling themselves that if my contribution could equal the dowry that I should normally have paid to take Agatha, they would no longer need, for their part, to spend a cent on the coming feast. This is a detail which will stick in my mind for a long time, in spite of king Solomon's precept, according to which the eyes should never look anywhere but on the side of life where the future lies.

The future was, for the moment, the child that Agatha was preparing to give me; and now, nobody was any longer in doubt that she really was expecting a child. One day, when I was sorting out my fishing gear for the next outing, Agatha said to me:

'Don't be too long coming back, this time . . .'

'What? You feel it coming already?' I asked.

'I tell you you must come back quickly. I want you to see him as soon as he's born.'

I promised to come back as soon as possible, and I left for the sea.

Splendid summer sun, sea now calm now rough, the absolute horizon of days which dawn and die, the thin distant plume of smoke from that boat the size of a grain of sand, gulls on the sunny shore, fine sand crunching under bare feet, dark green mangrove forests, huge oysters buried in the mud of the marshes, crocodiles taking flight at the noise of the paddles, wrecks floating on the silver-grey water, collections of enormous logs of wood, like foundations of gigantic lake cities, steamers growing bigger as you watch, fishing villages on the sandy banks, fish, mother-of-pearl fish, silver fish, smoked fish the colour of mahogany, fish dried on wattle, wrasse, suckers, sword-fish, fish of all kinds . . . evenings round the fire after a hard day and the rough sea, stories, songs, puzzles, proverbs, dances, dreams, smiling under the open sky, raffia mats on the ground, fraternity, solidarity, the sky, the sea, men, men lost in this overwhelming natural setting, simple men living to the sea's rhythm, under the watchful eye of millions of stars, men for God and for Satan, toiling for the lives of other men, their fellows, their brothers . . . that's what it's like, deep-sea fishing. I could travel the world and seek in vain for these kind of men. I am happy to know they are in my village, a step from my door, and that they meet me and speak to me from morning to evening, with their spirits fresh as the sea wind on purple evenings. Their life is an endless drama, between waves higher than a house of several stories, and the burning down of the fishing villages when carelessness or a wind from the wrong quarter brings catastrophe. And yet, for them, nothing is on an epic scale. The paddle is not a sword, the lament hummed over the calm waters does not have the sound of a legendary horn, fishing is not a battle, but a way of life. Happy life, what would I give to return to you again . . .

I promised Agatha that I would come home as quickly as possible. I kept my promise and returned to the village three weeks later.

During my absence, Maa Médi moved out of her own house; fearing that 'something' might happen while I was far away, she took up permanent residence at Agatha's. 'I have never seen greater devotion in my life,' said Fanny, touched by my mother's care for Agatha. And Maa Médi replied simply, with a smile: 'You haven't lived very long yet, my daughter . . . you'll see more before you reach my age . . .'

But fate is what it is.

I forgive it, even when I think that it was to me it chose to show 'more'. In fact, the day before I got back, Agatha's child had come into the world.

'He's beautiful, your son,' a woman on the bank said to me, while my mates and I were tying up the canoe in the green reeds.

'It's a boy?'

'Yes, a fine boy; he's better looking than you,' replied somebody else.

'And he's completely white . . .'

Then, all the people who had come to greet us began to laugh, to laugh in a way which did more than intrigue me.

'And then, so what?' asked my cousin Ekéké. 'He's completely white, he's completely white, and you start to laugh . . . what's funny about that? Aren't most children born completely white?'

I didn't understand either what it was all about, but I knew that my cousin was right. Most black children are born white, and only take on . . . local colour, a few days after coming into the world. So what was the meaning of this laughter? I ran to the village and went to see my child. He was there, lying in a large enamel bowl used as a cradle, wrapped in clothes which were quite unnecessary in the heat.

He was there, completely white, with long straight hair. Agatha looked at me and lowered her eyes. She didn't know what to say; neither did Maa Médi nor Fanny. None of them had expected a child as white as this. In the village, there was no end to conjectures about Agatha's child.

'A lot of black children are born like that . . .'

'As white as that? I've never seen . . .'

'Yes, yes, and then they change after a few days.'

'Very well, we shall see. I'll give you a month, if you like.'

A month, in a month I should know.

Once again, events were forcing me to turn my eyes to the future. 'When then shall I live in the present only?' I thought bitterly.

You will understand why this child, neither flesh nor fowl, which had just been born, made me so thoughtful, when I tell you the truth: the colour of my own skin is like the deepest shades of ebony. What's more, with my crinkly hair, my thick lips, and my nose with its somewhat generous base, I am sure that the *Nouveau Petit Larousse* of former times would not for a moment have hestitated to use me as a model for the black race. As for Agatha Moudio, very pretty as you know, she too was quite black, from head to foot. Definitely, it was very odd, this affair.

It was then that Mother Evil-Eye also added her grain of salt, and believe me, it was a big one:

'Perhaps,' she said, 'perhaps this child will one day have a mouthful of gold, like its father . . .'

I rushed to a mirror, on hearing this, and bared my teeth: two rows of ivory, clean and white beyond reproach. Then, still understanding nothing at all about it, I ran to Mother Evil-Eye's and bombarded her with questions. But she refused to give me any fuller explanations: 'You will see yourself, my child, you will see', was all she would say. Then, after a pause, 'Mother Eye, she sees everything, I can tell you, everything.'

So there was nothing left for me to do but to wait the ten days or a fortnight at the end of which Agatha's son would take on his final colour. I was even more generous: I kept on hoping for a whole month after the birth of the little boy, but his milk-chocolate complexion barely changed, or so little as to be hardly noticeable. Then, Mother Evil-Eye finally decided to speak:

'I saw her, your wife, when the big strong white man with gold teeth came to fetch her, at night, when you were away. He used to come on a bicycle, to avoid attracting attention. I saw him several times. But, son, what would you have had me say then? Wouldn't everybody have started talking about my evil tongue? So I refused to reveal what I saw. One day, your wife came home very late, in the early hours, and once again I saw the white man on his bicycle; he had come with her . . . don't inquire, and don't try to deceive yourself: Agatha's child is not yours, son.'

I went away, despondently, to tell king Solomon what I had just learned.

'What am I to do?' I asked him.

The king himself was no less embarrassed than I. But his proverbial wisdom helped him to find a solution, anywhere and at any time.

'What to do?' he repeated. 'Briefly, what are you to do with an illegitimate child? That's the point of your question, isn't it? And you want to make *me* answer? Come now, confess that you know better than me what to do: it's not the first "fatherless" child that you've had, as far as I know? So what did you do with the first?'

'But, king, it's not the same thing!'

'What? It's not the same thing? Tell me, what's not the same thing? The child? Or the way of producing it?'

I said nothing.

'Come now, son, pull yourself together,' continued the king; 'and then look things in the face. You haven't the right to let yourself be cast down like this, you, the Law, the strongest of our young men. And then, you know, whether it comes from heaven or hell, a child is still a child.'

So spoke king Solomon.

It's true.

Children, whether they come from the sin of hell, or from the best moulds of heaven, are all alike. They all descend from the same tree of life, the one whose branches demonstrate the insignificance of race, and their leaves the thousand characters of man. Later, they will become men and women, who love or hate each other, often without reason, bringing the same zeal to distinguish skin defects and to making classes of pariahs, as they would to trying to bring down the moon, when they have not yet finished reaping the fruits of the earth; they come into the world, all of them, graceful and beautiful, speaking the same dumb language of peace and friendship. Later, alas, they will speak the so much more noisy and stupid language of unreasonable reason, which leads to war and racialism. But long live the shining present of the angels, black or white or yellow or red, who, all in the same way, smilingly approach the shifting sands of life, and sing with the same innocent thirst the mother's milk of the first mornings of existence. Let them become later what they will become; so much the worse if they don't become real men, they will at least have been children.

Today, Agatha's son has grown. I didn't reject him, in spite of the terrible problem of conscience which he set me for some time after his birth. Naturally, with his appearance, he looks like a child come from afar. Sometimes I watch him playing in the village square, with small boys of his own age. Among them, he reminds me oddly of uncle Big-Heart's famous house, standing smartly among the modest straw huts of our village.

'You mustn't make comparisons like that!' king Solomon reproved me one day when he heard this reflection.

He is right. When all's said and done, Agatha's son expects from me, not the wicked and stupid sneer of a man deceived by fate, but the paternal advice which will bring him happiness in the strange adventure of life as a man. And, since I have come to understand this, I look back with loathing on the melancholy smile I still used to have sometimes, for long months after the birth of the child, when I remembered Maa Médi's predictions: 'My son,' she used to repeat, '*I* am telling you, that woman . . . she'll lead you a fine dance till you can't tell black from white.'